MW00571443

THE LEGACY

E. A. Briginshaw

E. A. Brigin
Oct 7/2015

Copyright © 2014 Ernest A. Briginshaw

All rights reserved. No part of this book may be used or reproduced by any means, graphic, electronic, or mechanical, including photocopying, recording, taping or by any information storage retrieval system without the express written permission of the author except in the case of brief quotations embodied in critical articles and reviews.

Graphic design work for the book cover completed by Nicole Hill. Images used on the book cover are licensed through Shutterstock. "Christ The Redeemer": Mark Schwettman / Shutterstock.com "Runners": Pavel L Photo and Video / Shutterstock.com

This is a work of fiction. All of the characters, names, incidents, organizations and dialogue in this novel are either the products of the author's imagination or are used fictitiously.

ISBN: 978-0-9921390-2-5 (Book)
ISBN: 978-0-9921390-3-2 (eBook)

ACKNOWLEDGMENTS

Although the novel is a work of fiction, some of the characters are composite characters based on my family and friends. Thanks to all of the people who reviewed and critiqued numerous drafts of this novel including friends, members of my family and writers from the London Writers Society. Special thanks to Nicole Hill for the graphic design of the images used on the book cover.

One of the fictional characters in this book, Tom Beamish, was named as a tribute to Maureen Beamish who passed away suddenly as the result of an accident in October 2012. Maureen worked for Legacy Partners of London Inc. and was always a warm and friendly person. She will be missed and remembered forever.

E. A. BRIGINSHAW

*** CHAPTER 1 ***

Eric Baxter gradually gained consciousness with a bad taste in his mouth, a mixture of blood and dirt. He spit the dirt out as he rolled over onto his back and felt the excruciating pain in his shoulder as he did so.

"Where am I?" he thought to himself.

The first light of daybreak came slithering through the canopy above him and it took a few seconds for his brain to comprehend what his eyes were seeing. The canopy was a huge brownish-green tarp that hung over make-shift poles that filled the room. His eyes followed the line of poles until they collided with the walls that were made out of a combination of barbed wire and chicken wire.

As the light grew, he realized he was not alone. Others lay in this dungeon with him. His eyes could barely focus but he recognized the body of his brother lying about thirty feet away. He tried to get up to check on him, but failed in his attempt. His mind was spinning as he tried to figure out where they were and how they got here. He continued to scan his surroundings until he saw the light reflect off the barrel of a rifle. The fear sliced through him like a knife as he started to recall the events of the last twenty-four hours. As he lost consciousness again, his mind drifted back to happier times.

*** CHAPTER 2 ***

Four months earlier...

Eric Baxter sat in the large auditorium with all of the other graduating students and strained his neck to try to see where his father and brother were sitting. However, he couldn't pick them out of the crowd of several hundred people who had come to see their loved ones receive their diplomas.

"Good afternoon everyone and welcome to the graduation ceremonies for the Business and Economics class of Fanshawe College," announced the master of ceremonies. "I'd like to begin by introducing our panel of distinguished presenters for today's ceremony."

Eric squirmed in his seat as he was already finding the graduation gown to be unbearably hot. He hoped the speeches wouldn't go on for too long before they started handing out the diplomas, but those hopes were quickly dashed when he heard the mayor introduced as one of the speakers. That meant that there would be no shortage of hot air being spewed into the room.

Out in the audience, Brian Baxter watched the proceedings with pride. Brian was in his mid-fifties and his grey hairs now out-numbered the black ones. He was tall and thin, in contrast to Eric who looked more like his mother's side of the family. Eric had floundered for several years after graduating high school floating from one dead-end job to the next. Brian wasn't sure this day would ever arrive but he knew that his wife never gave up hope that Eric would graduate from college. He wished she was still alive to see this, but Jean had passed away after a battle with cancer over five years ago. He would have to tell her all about it in their next conversation.

Brian looked at the empty chair on his right and wondered when his other son Charles, or Chip as he was more commonly known, would arrive. He showed up just as they were starting to hand out the diplomas.

"You're late," Brian said as he picked up the program he had placed on the vacant chair to hold the seat.

"I'm not late," Chip whispered. "I'm efficient. I didn't want to sit through all of those boring speeches and I got here just in time to see Eric get his diploma." Chip gave his father a reassuring smile.

"And now the graduates of the Business - Financial Planning program," said the master of ceremonies.

There were about thirty students majoring in Financial Planning and they all rose from their seats and started up the stairs to the stage. Brian grabbed his camera and raced down the aisle so he could get a picture of Eric as he was presented his diploma. When Eric saw him, he rolled his eyes in embarrassment, but the smile on his face showed it was a pretty big deal to him as well.

After the ceremony, all of the graduates gathered in the cafeteria for the reception, which easily spilled out onto the lawn outside of the building.

"Congratulations son," Brian said, giving Eric a hug.

"Thanks Dad."

Chip came forward and gave his brother a fist pump. "Hi Chip. I'm glad you came. I guess the next one of these will be when you graduate from Ohio State."

Chip had started attending the University of Waterloo a few years ago but had switched to Ohio State after they offered him a full athletic scholarship. Chip was twenty-three years old, three years younger than his brother. He was tall and thin like his father and a very good athlete. He specialized in long distance running, normally the 5,000 or 10,000 metre events, but he sometimes also competed in the 1,500 metre races. Brian had hoped that Chip would represent Canada in the upcoming Olympics, but Chip had applied to become a U.S. citizen a few years ago and they had fast-tracked his application so he could try out for the U.S. Olympic team. It had broken Brian's heart to hear that his son wouldn't be representing Canada, but Chip had said it would be easier to take advantage of the U.S. Olympic training program as they had a lot more money, which meant better coaches and training facilities.

Brian saw Tom Beamish among the crowd and waved him over to join them. Tom was in his early sixties and had been a close friend of Brian's for almost thirty years. Tom was also his investment advisor and had influenced Eric to pursue financial planning as his career.

"Congratulations," Tom said to Eric, giving him a firm handshake. "I heard you got the job with the bank."

"Yeah, thanks for all of your help," Eric said. "I started about a month ago and the people there seem really great. I'm not sure I would have got the job without you as a reference."

"No problem. I think working for a bank is the best fit for you at this stage of your career. I think you'd starve living off the commissions you'd get making sales for an investment broker."

Like several of his fellow graduates, Eric had been courted by a few of the big investment firms and their stories about how much money their representatives could make. Several of the graduates had been approached to bring twenty or more contacts with them to the interviews. Eric could easily come up with that many contacts, but most of them were in their twenties and like him, didn't have any money to invest.

Eric heard his name being called and saw several of his classmates gathering for a group photo. He thanked Tom again and headed off to be part of it. Chip headed off in the same direction, mostly because he noticed that there were several cute girls in Eric's class.

"So I presume you'll be moving your money over to the bank so that Eric can look after your investments," Tom said to Brian after they had left.

"Not to worry," Brian said. "I don't believe in having all of my money managed by just one person."

"Even if they're family?"

"Especially if they're family," Brian said, nudging Tom with his shoulder. "I'm planning to move the money that I have with Great West Life over to Eric so he can get his feet wet, but I'll be leaving most of my investments with you for a while yet. I really appreciate all of the advice you've given me over the years and for helping Eric get started in his career."

"I'll help him out whenever I can and I won't feel slighted if you want to move more and more of your money over to Eric to manage."

Tom had already been a mentor to several college students over the years and had been a guest lecturer at numerous classes, but he'd taken a special interest in Eric.

Tom had been in the business long enough to see the rise and fall of the markets several times over. He had seen a lot of financial advisors be there in the good times, but bail when the going got tough. He had a feeling that Eric would be there for his clients through thick and thin.

Eric and Chip came back over to tell their dad that they were heading off with some of the students for a post-graduation party. "We'll see you at Tony Roma's tomorrow night for your birthday supper," Eric said as they headed off. Brian was turning fifty-five and always liked to feast on a full rack of ribs on his birthday.

"Did you get dad a birthday present yet?" Chip asked Eric as they walked away.

"Yep, I got him one of those new Adams rescue golf clubs that he's been talking about, the ones that are supposed to make it easier to get the ball out of the rough. We saw it advertised on the Golf Channel a few weeks ago and dad was wondering if it would help his game. How about you?"

"I haven't got him anything yet, but I'll pick up something tomorrow before the dinner," Chip said.

The next day Chip was wandering through the mall looking for a present, but didn't see anything that he liked. He noticed a huge line-up at the lottery ticket booth and signs that said the jackpot had grown to $50 million dollars, plus ten additional bonus draws for $1 million each.

"That could work," Chip thought to himself. But he didn't want to wait in line as it didn't seem a very efficient use of his time. "That will be my backup plan," he thought. He continued to search the stores in the mall but the only thing he bought was a birthday card that had a funny picture of an old guy golfing and complaining that he couldn't find his balls anymore. As he was paying for the card, Chip heard the announcement that the stores would

7

soon be closing. He hustled back to the lottery ticket booth which now had no line-up at all and purchased a lottery ticket.

At supper that night, Brian and Eric both finished off a full rack of ribs. Chip barely ate half of his meal. "Is there something wrong with your ribs?" Brian asked Chip.

"No, they're fine. My gut is bothering me a bit. It's been bugging me for the last few weeks."

"Well, make sure you see a doctor to get everything checked out."

"I will," Chip said, but knew he wouldn't. He was sure it was just stress caused by the exams he had just written at Ohio State, plus worrying about the upcoming Olympic trials.

"Here's your birthday present," Eric said after they had finished the meal. Brian had already seen it was a golf club as it was impossible to gift-wrap, although he had taped a bow to the end of it.

"This is great," Brian said. "I've seen these advertised on TV and a few of the guys have said it really helps their golf game."

Chip gave his dad the birthday card with the lottery ticket inside. "Cute," Brian said when he read the card, "but I'm still young enough to know exactly where my balls are."

"I hope you win the $50 million," Chip said.

"This is actually for next week's draw," Brian said, "not tonight's draw. When did you buy the ticket?"

"Just before I came for dinner. Why would they sell me a ticket for next week's draw?"

"You must have missed the cut-off time to get into tonight's draw. Not to worry, I wouldn't know what to do with $50 million anyway."

"Speaking of money," Eric said. "Did you get a chance

to look at that investor profile questionnaire I gave you? I really need you to complete it before I can invest any of your money."

"No, not yet," Brian replied. "But I'll take a look at it over the next few days."

They finished their meal which included a small birthday cake that the boys had secretly snuck into the restaurant. Their server didn't seem to mind. In fact, she added a sparkler and had several of the other servers join in to sing happy birthday, much to Brian's embarrassment.

* * *

The next evening Brian sat down at his dining room table and opened the investor profile questionnaire that Eric had given him. It was quite comprehensive, much more so than anything Brian had ever seen before. Rather than being intrusive, it actually gave Brian more confidence that they'd be managing his money based on his requirements rather than just trying to sell him mutual funds and generating sales commissions. The first few questions were fairly typical.

"How old are you?" Brian ticked the box that indicated he was between 50 and 65 years old.

"What is your estimated net worth?" Brian ticked the box indicating his net worth was over one million dollars. He started jotting down some figures and calculated that it was about $8.5 million. He had owned and operated several successful businesses and led a conservative lifestyle so he didn't spend much, relatively speaking. And Tom had managed his investments quite well, contributing significantly to the growth over the years.

Brian completed several more pages of the questionnaire. Some of the questions were hard to answer, forcing him to think for quite a while before making a choice. One of the last questions was the most interesting.

"Please rate the relative importance of each of the following objectives on a scale from one to ten, with one being the least important and ten being the most important."

Brian gave the *"Maximum Growth"* category a rating of two as he felt that he had saved more than enough money already to live comfortably. He gave the *"Security"* section a rating of eight as he didn't feel comfortable taking a lot of risk with his investments. He continued through the questionnaire filling in his ratings for several more categories.

The last one was titled *"Leaving a Legacy"* and Brian didn't hesitate at all. He immediately gave that a rank of ten.

*** CHAPTER 3 ***

Eric sat in his office at the bank reviewing the questionnaire that his father had provided him. He had been working at the bank for just over a month and had gone through the initial consultation with only about a dozen clients so far. The first few had been done in partnership with the senior financial planner for the region who had sat in on the meetings in case Eric came across something he didn't know how to handle. Since then, Eric had successfully handled the meetings on his own, but his boss would be sitting in on this meeting as well. The bank's policy prevented Eric from handling matters for family members without having a supervisor sign off on everything to prevent any conflict of interest. Tom Beamish would also be sitting in on the meeting. Eric was nervous knowing that his mentor, his boss, and more importantly, his father, would be watching his every move. He was surprised to find that he felt more nervous now than he had when he'd written the Certified Financial Planner exams. Eric took a deep breath and headed out to the waiting room.

"Hi Dad. Hello Mr. Beamish." He showed them the

way to his office and invited them to sit down.

"Pretty big office," Brian said teasingly. "Tom, how many years were you in the business before you got an office this big?"

"My office still isn't this big," Tom said.

"This is just temporary," Eric said, somewhat embarrassed. "I'll be moving into the smaller office across the hall next week when Bob leaves. He's been transferred to the Kitchener branch. They're just letting me use the regional manager's office until then."

Just then, the regional manager came into the office and introduced himself. He had known Tom Beamish for over ten years but had never met Brian before. "Don't mind me, I'll just sit in the back and monitor things," the regional manager said.

Eric invited Brian and Tom to sit down at a small table in the corner of the office. "Thanks for completing the investor profile. I just have a few additional questions." Eric laid out the pages of the questionnaire in front of them. "I noticed that most of your money is invested in Canada and the United States, with only a fraction invested in Europe, Asia and South America. Given the size of your portfolio, is there a reason that you're avoiding those parts of the world?"

"I just don't feel comfortable investing in parts of the world that I don't know much about," Brian said.

"I've been trying to get your dad to consider diversifying to more international investments," Tom said, "but you know how stubborn he can be."

Eric just smiled, thinking it best not to comment on his father's stubborn streak. "Okay, I understand that you want to move the money you've got with Great West Life over to our bank. I noticed that money is currently held in segregated funds. Why have you got that money in seg funds?"

"That money goes back quite a few years," Brian said. "That's when I was starting up one of my companies out west, before you were born. There was always a risk that things wouldn't work out and I wanted to ensure that some of my investments were protected from creditors. I consider that my retirement money, not much, but enough to meet my basic needs. Tom looks after the investments for everything else."

"Are you sure that's enough money to meet your basic needs?" Eric asked. "There's less than four hundred thousand dollars sitting there. I'd suggest you create a budget showing your needs and your wants in your retirement years."

Tom smiled. He remembered the lecture that he had given at Eric's school covering that exact topic and was glad to see that Eric had been listening. Many financial planners based their estimate of retirement requirements as a percentage of the client's income before they retired, but Tom was not a big fan of that approach. He much preferred creating a budget. It also forced his clients to start thinking about what they wanted to do in their retirement years.

"Already done," Brian said as he handed his budget to Eric. "Tom asks me to update it every year in case something changes, and it has. My expenses have dropped considerably since you and your brother moved out on your own and I'm not much for living extravagantly." Although he was now pretty wealthy, Brian continued to live in the same mid-sized house they had purchased when they had moved to London Ontario when Eric was about ten years old.

Eric was still a little concerned that his father was underestimating his basic needs, but decided to let it slide for the time-being. "Okay, last question," Eric said. "I noticed that you ranked leaving a legacy as your most important objective. What exactly do you mean by leaving a legacy?"

"It **is** my most important objective," Brian said, "and a good financial advisor should know what that means."

Eric felt his face flush a little bit. He knew what leaving a legacy meant, but he needed more specifics from his father. "Do you want to leave money to a university or a hospital?"

"No, I'm not looking for anyone to name a park or the wing of a hospital after me."

"Are you looking to set up a trust fund for Chip and myself?" Eric felt embarrassed even asking the question.

Brian chuckled. "Nope. You and your brother will get the money from my life insurance policy but it's up to you guys to make your own money."

Eric still looked confused. Tom knew exactly what Brian's legacy was and was about to explain it to Eric, but Brian cut him off.

"Well son, I guess they didn't teach you everything at school after all," Brian said. "It looks like you've got some research to do."

* * *

Later that night, Brian struggled to get to sleep. He turned on the TV and watched the Late Show but still wasn't sleepy, so he read for a while after that until he finally drifted off.

"Why didn't you just tell Eric what your legacy is?" Jean asked.

Brian recognized the scolding tone in his wife's voice. She had been dead for over five years now, but she still showed up periodically in Brian's dreams, usually when she wasn't happy with him.

"You can't just hand everything to him on a platter," Brian said.

"Why not?"

"Because it's not good for him. He's got to figure some things out for himself."

"Well, as parents, it's up to us to put them on the right path when we think they need it."

"What about them finding their own path? We can't be there for them forever."

"Wanna bet? I'm still here with you and I've been dead for five years. I can haunt you forever."

"Whatever happened to *till death do us part?*"

"Good luck with that!!! You should know me better than that by now. But I guess I should let you get some sleep or else you're no use to anyone."

"Yes, letting me get some sleep would be much appreciated." Brian remembered how his wife would wake him up in the middle of the night to talk if something was on her mind. He usually just gave in so he could get back to sleep. "I love you – goodnight," Brian said, hoping this would end the conversation.

"I love you too. By the way, check up on Chip. There's something going on with him and I think he needs our help."

*** CHAPTER 4 ***

Chip kicked his leg out and then carefully placed it into the starting blocks. In the crouched position, his gut seemed to hurt even more than normal. He'd never gone to see a doctor about the pain and it had gotten worse over the last few weeks.

This event was the 1,500 metre Olympic trials and was more of a sprint than the 5,000 or 10,000 metre distances. Chip had already made the U.S. Olympic team for those events, but he thought he had a realistic chance at this distance as well because he was pretty quick in addition to having the endurance of a long distance runner. The starting gun sounded and Chip's gut felt like someone had sliced him open as he exploded out of the blocks. After the first 200 metres, he was already a few paces behind and it was becoming apparent to him that he wasn't capable of making up any ground. By the time he reached the finish line, he was in agony.

Later that night, the pain was becoming unbearable so Chip headed into the emergency department at the hospital. "On a scale from one to ten, how much pain are you in right now?" Dr. Fleming asked. The emergency room doctor didn't look much older than Chip.

"Probably about a seven," Chip answered. "I think I might have an ulcer."

The doctor was reviewing the notes made by the triage nurse when Chip had first arrived at the hospital and noted that Chip had a slight fever. He put down the chart and pulled on some medical gloves to begin the examination. "How about when I press on your abdomen?" he asked as he gently pushed on different parts of Chip's stomach. There was some tenderness but no real pain.

Suddenly, Chip let out a yell when the doctor pushed on a spot in his lower abdomen. "That would be a ten, right there," Chip gasped.

"I'm going to send you for a CT-scan," the doctor said. "I'm worried that it could be your appendix."

Chip hadn't even considered that, but it made sense the more he thought about it. The doctor also ordered some blood work. Chip laid in the bed hoping that it wasn't his appendix because he was sure that any kind of surgery would jeopardize his participation in the Olympics. As the time passed, Chip became more and more worried. He knew he had been kidding himself thinking it was only an ulcer. He wished he had taken his father's advice and had it checked out earlier.

It was over three hours later when Dr. Fleming returned with the results. "I've got some good news and some bad news."

"Give me the good news first," Chip said.

"Well, the good news is that your appendix is fine. The bad news is that we think you've got Crohn's disease."

Chip had never heard of it, but it didn't sound good. "Is that something you can give me some pills for?"

"I can give you something to manage the pain. We

17

E. A. BRIGINSHAW

believe you've got a small abscess in your lower bowel which is causing the pain and I can prescribe you some antibiotics to treat the infection. But Crohn's is a complicated disease and there is no simple treatment or cure. We'd like to schedule you for a colonoscopy and put you on some corticosteroids to treat the inflammation."

Chip didn't understand everything the doctor had said but the mention of steroids immediately raised a red flag. "I'm an athlete and I just qualified for the Olympics. I can't take any drugs that are going to jeopardize me competing. The Olympics are only a few weeks away. Is there anything you can do to keep me healthy without destroying my chances at competing?"

"I'm not sure," the doctor said. "I'll have to consult with the specialists in the gastroenterology department before deciding on the best course of action." The doctor could see the panic in Chip's eyes. "We call them the gut doctors," he said trying to ease the tension. "They like dealing with this kind of shit." His attempt at humour wasn't working. "Do you have the contact information for your team doctors?"

Chip pulled a card from his wallet that had the names and numbers of several people associated with the Olympic program and gave it to the doctor.

"Try not to worry," the doctor said as he scanned the information on the card. "I'm confident we'll come up with a solution that works for you."

It was a few more hours until Dr. Fleming returned again, this time accompanied by another doctor. "This is Dr. Kachmarsky," he said, "one of the top gut doctors in the country."

"Don't be a suck-up," Dr. Kachmarsky said, "but I'm not **one** of the top gut doctors in the country, I'm **the** top gut doctor." Both doctors sensed that Chip was bracing himself for bad news. "Cheer up," Dr. Kachmarsky said. "I've consulted with your team doctors and prescribed some pain killers and some antibiotics, neither of which will jeopardize your chances of competing. We've delayed the colonoscopy and any long term treatment of the disease until after the Olympics."

"I'll still be able to compete, right?" Chip asked.

"You can, provided it doesn't get any worse," Dr. Kachmarsky said. "There's only a few days' worth of pain killers so they will have cleared your system in time. If the antibiotics work, then the infection should clear up as well. But don't kid yourself, this is a very serious disease and will get worse if we don't take some kind of action in the long-term."

The doctor gave him some pamphlets with more information on Crohn's, but suggested there was more detailed and current information available online. He also put Chip on a specialized diet which would hopefully reduce the chances of another flare-up of the disease, but there was no guarantee.

When Chip got home, he scoured the internet for more information. He read that it is an inflammatory bowel disease that is usually first diagnosed in people in their teens or early twenties. "Why me?" Chip thought to himself. He didn't smoke or drink, ate all of the right foods and obviously got lots of exercise. He continued reading to see that it is classified as an immune deficiency disease that affects about 600,000 people in North America with no known cure. "Why had he never heard of it before?" Chip asked himself. He read about the drugs available to control it, but some of those drugs seemed to have side effects which could be worse than the disease itself. The more he read, the more worried he became. He closed his laptop. He decided he would deal with it after the Olympics.

Over the next few weeks, Chip continued to train with the others who had qualified for the Olympics, but his times were getting worse rather than better. He had lost over ten pounds and was finding it difficult to find the energy to train hard.

"Your times are going to have to improve," Coach McDonald yelled at Chip after their latest training session. "This is not the time to start taking it easy."

"I know," Chip said, hanging his head as he slumped over to the bench to take off his track shoes.

"Don't worry about it," said Michael Porter, Chip's training partner. He would also be competing in the 5,000 and 10,000 metre events. Michael was several years older than Chip and was the consummate professional. He had competed in the last two Olympics, winning a bronze medal in the first and a silver in the second. He was hoping to win the gold this time.

"The coach's job is to keep pushing us as hard as he can," Michael whispered. "Don't take him too seriously."

"I don't," Chip replied, "but he's right. My times are getting worse and worse."

"There's no point burning yourself out now," Michael said as he put his hand on Chip's shoulder. "The goal is to peak at the Olympics."

Chip and Michael had grown quite close over the last few weeks, even though they had never met before the Olympic trials. In some ways, they were like soldiers in the trenches preparing for a big battle, watching each other's back. Chip admired Michael's calmness.

"Remember, we're just men playing kid's games," Michael said. "Just do the best you can. No one is going to live or die based on whether we win or lose the race."

Later that night, Chip called his father. "How are you doing son?"

"Okay, but not great. I don't have a lot of energy and I can tell the coaches are concerned about my times."

"Well Crohn's can suck a lot of energy out of you." Brian had also been doing a lot of research about the disease ever since Chip had called him after being in the hospital. "There's nothing more important than your health, so it's okay to pull out if you don't think you can make it."

"Yeah, I know, but I want to compete if I can. I've been training for this for years."

Brian could hear the depression in Chip's voice and tried to talk about something more exciting. "Eric and I received our Olympic tickets yesterday and we're both excited about going to Rio de Janeiro."

Brian and Eric would be heading down earlier than Chip as they were taking a few days to see several of the events. Chip's schedule was dictated by the team. The athletes would be arriving just two days before their events and moving into the Olympic Village. Athletes who had competed in earlier events would be vacating their rooms in the village so the newly arriving athletes could take their spots. Security was strictly controlled.

"I've only ever seen the Olympics on TV," Brian said, "and I've never been to Rio. Eric wants to stay for another week after the Olympics are over to do some sightseeing."

"Yeah, he told me," Chip said. "I'm planning to take a bit of a vacation after the events as well. I'm sure I'll need some time to relax by that point." He didn't know that it would be a long time until he could relax again.

*** CHAPTER 5 ***

The following week Brian stopped into the bank to sign the forms to transfer his holdings from Great West Life over to the bank for Eric to manage.

"Okay, this part of the form describes where we're going to place your money," Eric said to his father. "We're going to put thirty-five percent of the money into a Canadian equity fund, another thirty-five percent into an international balanced fund, twenty percent into long-term bonds and ten percent into short-term bonds."

"I'm not sure that I want that much in an international fund," Brian said. "Remember, we talked about how I don't like investing in places I know nothing about. I don't understand how the business and government works in a lot of these countries."

"Not to worry," Eric said. "Although it's called an international fund, seventy percent is invested in U.S. companies with the balance invested in stable companies spread around the world, companies you've probably already heard of. It's the best way to start to diversify your holdings without taking on too much risk."

Brian looked at the information Eric had given him describing the international fund and saw the list of companies they invested in. Eric was right. They were all major companies that Brian recognized. "Did you talk to Tom about this?"

"Yes, he agrees with my strategy."

Brian was still a little worried but decided he should just take the advice he had been given. He trusted them completely.

Eric pulled out some brochures with information about estates, trust funds and creating a legacy. They were filled with pictures of forests, buildings, monuments and smiling people gazing to the skies. Eric knew it was mostly fluffy promotional material, but the back of one of the brochures had a page that listed the seven steps to creating a legacy. "Here's some information about creating a legacy," Eric said. "Once you've reviewed it, we can sit down and start putting together a plan."

Brian smiled. "My plan is already in place, but you haven't figured out what it is yet, have you?"

"Not a clue," Eric confessed.

"Okay, I'll make a deal with you. We'll talk about it after we get back from the Olympics. If you haven't figured it out by your mother's birthday, I'll explain it to you at her dinner."

Brian continued to have a dinner on his wife's birthday every year. It was something they had done every year when she was alive and Brian saw no reason to stop when she passed away. Eric and Chip both knew it was mandatory that they attend, no excuses accepted.

"Deal," Eric said. Perhaps his father had just thrown him a clue. He had been trying to figure out what his father wanted his legacy to be, but maybe he should have been looking at what his mother wanted instead. She was always

23

the one who worried more about the future.

That night Eric was wracking his brain trying to figure it out. He was looking through an old family album hoping that the pictures would provide a clue. There were numerous pictures of the whole family out at the lake in Saskatchewan. They had lived out west when he was little, having moved to Ontario when his father had expanded one of his businesses. Those were definitely happy times, but the pictures didn't provide any clues as to a legacy.

Eric continued to page through the album. He came across some pictures of his mother with several of her friends out in the Rockies. He squinted to try to see what was written on the tee-shirts they were all wearing. "Banff Babes," Eric said to himself when he figured it out. He smiled as he remembered the ladies that his mother used to sing with in choirs in Edmonton and Calgary. He recognized one of the ladies because she used to give him piano lessons when he was a kid. He pulled the picture out of the album and turned it over and saw that the date on the picture indicated it was taken only a few months before his mother had passed away. It also had a note from one of the ladies that said *"Email me so we can start planning next year's trip"* and it showed her email address.

"I wonder if those ladies knew what my mother wanted her legacy to be?" Eric thought to himself. He knew those ladies talked about things they would never talk to anyone else about. He pulled out his laptop and started composing the email to ask.

After he sent the email, Eric started searching the internet for information about the Olympics. He would be heading down to Brazil with his father in two days and was getting more and more excited about the trip. He would be just one of the thousands of people watching the competitions and Eric couldn't imagine how excited Chip must be knowing that he would be competing.

* * *

Brian and Eric sat in the lounge outside of gate E20 in the Houston airport waiting for their flight down to Rio de Janeiro. They had already spent over three hours flying from Toronto to Houston and the next leg of the journey would be over ten hours, so their enthusiasm about going to the Olympics was starting to wane. Although they had flown economy class on the first leg of the trip, Brian was glad that they'd decided to fly first-class on the second leg.

"Would you like a glass of champagne?" the stewardess asked shortly after they had boarded, "or would you like to try one of our hors d'oeuvres?"

"No thanks," Brian said. Eric also declined. They weren't flying first-class to take advantage of the fancy food or free drinks. First class allowed them to take advantage of the flat-bed seats that could fully recline to over six feet in length so they could sleep on the overnight flight. Despite that, they both had trouble sleeping and found themselves wide awake at 5:00 a.m.

"Do you think Chip has a realistic chance of winning a medal?" Eric asked his father.

"Well, he's never been ranked higher that twelfth in the world," Brian said, "but there's always upsets at the Olympics, so you never know. I just hope he enjoys the experience. Not very many people ever get to say they've competed in the Olympics."

"The last time I spoke to him, he sounded really stressed out. I think he's worried about letting people down."

"Yeah, I know, but he shouldn't," Brian said. "I think the Crohn's is taking a toll on him as well. He's always been so confident, even cocky, but I think he's starting to realize he's not Superman after all."

The *"Fasten Seat Belt"* sign flashed on, so they knew they were starting to get close to landing. Eric looked out the window on his side of the plane but all he could see was water. As the plane banked, the city came into view.

"What's that?" Eric asked, pointing to a huge statue.

"Christ the Redeemer." Brian had been reading about some of the tourist attractions during the flight. "I read where it's one of the largest statues in the world." For sure, it was impressive. Brian wasn't a religious man but just looking at this statue somehow felt inspiring about great things to come.

"I know practically nothing about this place," Eric confessed, "but it's much bigger and more modern than I was expecting."

"It's a huge city," Brian said. "But I've been reading that it's a mixture of modern buildings for the rich and favelas, or shanty towns, for the poor. For the Olympics, I'm sure they'll be steering us away from the poorer parts of the city."

Eric scanned the impressive looking city. He could also see how quickly the landscape changed from modern city to dense jungle just outside of the city limits. "Oh, Chip and I registered for that tour you recommended after the Olympics. It's supposed to include a tour of the whole city and some of the rest of Brazil as well."

"Glad to hear it," Brian said. "I feel a lot better knowing you guys will be on a tour bus rather than just trekking around on your own."

The stewardess came through the cabin and asked the passengers to prepare for landing. After they had landed and gone through customs, Brian and Eric found the shuttle that would take them to the Sheraton. It was a five-star hotel, but wasn't as ritzy as places like the Copacabana, one of the top-rated hotels in Rio. When they got to their room, they both crashed for the rest of the day to recover from their long flight.

*** CHAPTER 6 ***

The sun still wasn't up when Maria Silva rose from her bed in Rochina de Favela. The building that she lived in swayed in the wind. She was convinced a strong wind would blow the whole thing over some day, along with all of the other makeshift buildings in the favela. She heard the jet fly overhead as yet another plane-load of Olympic tourists arrived and wondered how her mother could continue to sleep.

As she watched her sleep, Maria could see that her mother had once been a real beauty, but that was before life had beaten her down. Maria had never known her father. Talk was that her father had been one of the drug lords who controlled the favela, or did until he was murdered. Some people said he had been killed by a rival gang member, but Maria had also heard the whispers that her mother had done the deed herself. Maria had asked her mother once, and only once, whether the story was true. She still had the mark by her left ear where her mother had hit her.

Maria looked at herself in the mirror. She could still see

the scar on the side of her face, despite the poor light in the room and the numerous cracks in the mirror. She pulled her long black hair forward to hide the scar. But the mirror also showed that Maria had inherited her mother's beauty. She slipped on the dress that revealed every supple curve in her body, debating how many buttons on the front to leave undone. She decided the more conservative route would be best this morning.

She quietly closed the door and started her walk to work at the Copacabana. She wasn't on the official payroll of the hotel, but had an arrangement with the maître d' that she could work there just for tips. She had a similar arrangement with the bartender at night.

"Take these to table twelve," Lorenzo said when he saw her arrive. "They've been waiting for quite a while."

Maria took a quick glance at table twelve and saw a family of four, with the mother and father trying to entertain their kids who were obviously getting restless. The clothes they wore indicated they were rich, as were all of the patrons at the Copacabana. She quickly loaded up her tray with their order, stole some fresh fruit and some croissants from another order that was waiting to be delivered, and headed off.

"I'm terribly sorry for the delay," Maria said in flawless English. The staff had been told to speak English at work as it made the customers feel more comfortable. "We've included some fresh fruit and some croissants, courtesy of the hotel." Before she gave the kids their meals, she rearranged the fruit so they showed a happy-face on their plates.

"Cool," giggled the kids in delight when they saw them.

She complimented the lady at how pretty her dress was when she placed her meal on the table. "Oh, I'm so glad you like it," the lady said as she reached over and touched her husband's arm. "Jean-Pierre bought it for me yesterday."

"You have very fine taste," Maria said to the man. When she picked up the plates after they had finished their meal, Maria could see how appreciative they were in the generous tip they left. They also left a note saying "Thanks for taking care of us while in your beautiful country" signed by Jean-Pierre and Sylvia Girard. Maria sighed as she dreamed about the life they must have.

"Could you take the order at table eighteen," Lorenzo said, interrupting Maria's daydream. Maria looked over at the table and saw six men, probably in their mid-twenties or early thirties. She undid a couple of buttons at the top of her dress and a few more at the bottom and headed over.

"What can I interest you in today?" she said when she arrived. She leaned in to take their order as if she was having trouble hearing them. She wasn't wearing a bra, which was easily noticed by each of the men as they placed their order. As she served their meals, Maria continued to flirt with them.

"We'll be back again tomorrow," they said when they were leaving the restaurant. One of the men kissed her hand as he was leaving, slipping her a crisp U.S. $50 bill when he did so.

Maria knew exactly how to work a room to obtain the biggest tips - when to be totally conservative and professional, and when to be a little more provocative. She didn't have to deliver sex to make money. There were plenty of women in Rio ready and willing to do that. But Maria had learned that she could make more money providing the anticipation of sex rather than actually delivering it.

After the breakfast rush was over, Maria walked back home with her tips held in her hand. You would think that she would be an easy mark, walking through the favela with a wad of cash in her hand. But no one ever touched Maria. It was understood by everyone that she was untouchable. When she arrived back home, she placed the money on the table.

"Is that all you got?" her mother asked.

*** CHAPTER 7 ***

A few days later, Chip and Michael looked out of the window as their plane descended into Rio. Chip's mind was racing with the anticipation of his upcoming events in the Olympics. "The Olympics" he said to himself. Just saying it caused his heart to flutter.

All of the U.S. athletes were seated together in the same section of the plane and the coach had spoken to them several times during the flight about the importance of having their security credentials with them at all times. Sadly, the Olympics were a perfect target for terrorists.

"Please keep any information about your identification pass completely confidential," Coach McDonald warned. "At the London Olympics in 2012, several athletes innocently posted pictures of their ID passes, including the barcode, on their Facebook pages. While I know you all want to keep your family and fans up-to-date on your Olympic experience, this is extremely dangerous. In London, it didn't take long for some of these fake IDs to start appearing at the venues. Remember, all of this security is there to protect you."

"I remember that," Michael whispered to Chip, recalling his experience in London. "One of the British athletes tweeted out a picture of himself posing with his identification pass. It caused a security nightmare."

As the athletes disembarked the plane, they were led down a special hallway separate from the rest of the passengers. Their IDs were scanned by electronic readers when they entered the hallway and again when they boarded the bus which would take them to the Olympic Village where all of the athletes, trainers and coaches were being housed. There were the normal security personnel that you would see at any airport, but there were also armed military personnel at every entrance and exit. Chip felt intimidated by all of the fully automatic weapons that were on display.

As he stepped off the bus at the Olympic Village, his ID was scanned again. He was alarmed when the reader flashed a red light and a buzzer sounded.

"Sir, would you please step to the side," the security agent said to Chip. Immediately, Chip saw several guns pointed in his direction and he froze in his spot. "Have you had any problems with this pass at any of the other checkpoints?" the agent asked.

"No," Chip croaked. The lump in his throat was so large that he could hardly speak. He cleared his throat before continuing. "They scanned it when I was at the airport and before I got on the bus. This is the first problem that I've had."

"Have you been in possession of your security pass the entire time?" the agent asked.

"Yes, it's been around my neck the whole time," Chip replied.

The security agent wiped the pass on his shirt-sleeve and attempted to scan it again. This time it flashed green. "Sometimes they just pick up a little dirt. You may proceed."

The guns pointed in Chip's direction were lowered to let him pass, but he felt the eyes of the soldiers continue to monitor his every movement. Chip was sure that he didn't take another breath until he stepped through the door of his room at the Olympic Village. The room reminded him of his dorm room at the residence at Ohio State and he was pleased that he would be sharing it with Michael.

"It kind of makes you feel like you're in prison, doesn't it?" Michael said as he threw his gear into the corner of the room, "but it's actually for our own protection."

"Yeah, I suppose so," Chip said, "but I may have wet myself a little bit when they pointed those guns at me." Michael laughed, but Chip knew it was pretty close to the truth.

"Now that we're inside the Olympic Village, you can relax a bit," Michael said, "but you should be prepared for that every time we leave to go to one of our events. I've been through this a few times now. You'll get used to it. After a while, you'll come to feel safer when the security guys are around. When they're not there, that's when you should start looking over your shoulder."

After getting settled in their room, Chip and Michael headed down to the common room which was filled with athletes from the various countries. They headed into one of the side rooms which had numerous computers available for their use. Chip felt a lot more relaxed among all of the other athletes.

"Hey, could you take a picture of us?" Chip asked one of the other competitors. "I want to post it on my Facebook page."

The other athlete didn't understand English very well, but "Facebook" seemed to be the same in any language, so he got the gist of what was being asked. Chip and Michael posed for the picture, both making sure they covered their IDs for the photo.

"Are you going to post a picture for all of your admirers?" Michael teased.

"Yeah, both of them," Chip answered. "I told my dad and my brother that I'd be posting things so we could keep in touch." Although they were all now in the same city, the security around the Olympics made it practically impossible for Chip to see his brother or his father in person.

Chip and Michael scanned the room looking for a computer that wasn't being used, but every one of them was taken. Chip headed over to stand behind a girl who looked like she might be getting close to finishing.

"I'll be a few more minutes," the girl said when she became aware that someone was hovering over her shoulder. She pulled the computer in a little closer so that Chip couldn't see what she was typing on the screen.

"No problem," Chip said. "Take your time." He took a step back to give her a bit more privacy. She had long blonde hair which she had pulled to the side which revealed a slender neck that Chip couldn't help but notice had a small tattoo of a red maple leaf on it. "What part of Canada are you from?" Chip asked.

"Kitchener," she replied.

"I'm from London," Chip said.

She turned around and smiled, but raised one eyebrow when she saw the USA team logo on the shirt Chip was wearing. "Really? All evidence to the contrary."

Chip shrugged. "Yeah, I'm actually competing for the U.S. team because I moved to the States to go to Ohio State, but I was born and raised in Canada. My dad and brother still live there."

"Traitor," she said as she turned back to her keyboard.

Chip found himself really attracted to this girl, so didn't

want to just give up. "So, what events are you competing in?"

"Women's hurdles, both the 100 metre and 400 metre events."

"I'm competing in the 5K and 10K events," Chip said, but he wasn't sure she heard him, or even cared.

"It's all yours," she said as she logged off the computer and rose from her chair.

"I'm Chip Baxter," he said as he extended his hand.

"Robin," she said, shaking his hand. She didn't give her last name.

"I hear they're giving tours of the facilities to the athletes later on tonight," Chip said. "Are you interested in going on one of them?"

"My teammates and I are already registered for the tour starting at 6:45," Robin answered. "Maybe I'll see you then."

"Great," Chip said. "I'll be sure to be there." Chip watched as she walked over to join her teammates.

Michael still hadn't found an available computer so he headed over to use the same one that Chip had found. "My, she's a healthy looking girl," Michael said as he approached.

Chip knew exactly what he meant. "Yes, she is put together extremely well," he sighed.

Chip sat down at the computer and uploaded the picture of himself and Michael to his Facebook page. After posting his update, Chip checked his brother's Facebook page and saw a picture of Eric and their dad standing outside of the Sheraton hotel, so Chip knew they had also made it to Rio safe and sound.

Michael uploaded the same picture of Chip and himself to his own Facebook page. "That's not for my fans," he explained. "It's just so my mom and dad can see what's going on," Michael said. "They wanted to come but it's pretty expensive and I was worried about all of the news about potential terrorist attacks, so I told them to stay at home this time. Besides, they've already seen me compete at the last two Olympics."

* * *

Later that day, Michael stood waiting for Chip. "Didn't you say you were meeting that girl at 6:45?" Michael asked. "You've literally got one minute to get dressed and over to where the tour starts."

Chip had just stepped out of the shower. He was going to be late, as usual. "Could you head over there and tell her I'm on my way?"

"I'll try," Michael said, "but no guarantees."

It was almost fifteen minutes later when Chip showed up and saw Michael leaning up against a pillar in the common room. "Did Robin not show up?" Chip asked.

"Yeah, she's come and gone," Michael answered. "You've got to realize girls like that won't wait around for your sorry ass. Robin and her teammates headed off with some guys from Australia, and given that one of those guys was already sporting a medal, I think you just blew any chance you had with that girl."

* * *

The next morning, Chip and Michael boarded a bus to take them to one of the training sites which was located in another part of the city. There were no fans allowed at this track as it was only used by the Olympic athletes for training, not competing. Still, security was strictly controlled with only the athletes and their coaches allowed access.

Chip and Michael were there for a few hours doing wind sprints and various other training exercises. At this stage, it was important to stay loose and not do anything that could potentially cause an injury.

As they were finishing up their training session, Chip noticed some female hurdlers having their own training session on the other side of the track. He headed over to get a closer look and was pleased to see that it was the Canadian team. He picked out Robin right away, despite her having her long blonde hair pulled into a pony-tail. He waved at her, but he wasn't sure she saw him.

"Chip, it's time to go," Michael yelled from the other side of the field.

Chip was hoping to be able to apologize for being late the previous day, but it didn't look like he was going to get the chance. "Coming," Chip yelled back.

As they were gathering up their gear to get ready to leave, Chip suddenly became alarmed. "Hey, have you seen my security pass?" he asked Michael as he rifled through everything in the bag he had brought with him. "I'm sure I placed it in my bag before I did my wind sprints." Chip was starting to panic as he knew how important it was. He dumped everything in his bag out on the grass in the infield of the track, but his ID wasn't there.

"Here it is, over here," Michael yelled. Michael was sitting over near one of the benches taking off his track shoes. "It was just lying on the ground by the bench."

"How did it get over there?" Chip asked. "I wasn't anywhere close to that bench."

Michael sensed the panic in Chip's voice. "It's okay," he said. "Somebody probably just picked up your bag by mistake and it fell out when he carried it over to the bench. These bags all look the same."

Chip looked at the bags that were scattered around the infield and realized they all looked similar. "I suppose you're right."

However, Chip was even more nervous than normal when his pass was scanned when he boarded the bus to take them back to the Olympic Village and relieved when he saw the green light flash.

"You may proceed," the security agent said.

*** CHAPTER 8 ***

It was about 10 a.m. the next morning when Chip and Michael boarded the shuttle bus that would take them from the athlete's village to the Olympic stadium. It was only about a twenty minute drive and their race wasn't for another three hours, but they both wanted to get there early. As they were going through security at the stadium, Chip's badge once again set off the alarm.

"Sir, please step over to the side," the security agent said.

"It's probably just dirty," Chip tried to explain. "I had trouble with it a couple of days ago and it worked again once they cleaned it off."

The security agent cleaned Chip's security pass and scanned it again, but it still flashed red and sounded the alarm.

"I'm competing today," Chip pleaded. "I really need to get into the stadium."

"According to the error code from the scanner, it indicates that this ID has already been used to enter the stadium. Have you entered the facilities any time earlier today?"

"No," Chip said. "We've just arrived on the shuttle bus from the Olympic Village."

"Have you been in possession of your security pass the entire time?"

Chip thought back to the incident the day before at the training facility when he had found his ID badge lying on the ground. When he told the security agent, the agent immediately stepped away and reported the incident to the rest of the security team over his walkie-talkie. Suddenly there was a flurry of activity and chatter.

"I'm sorry sir, but you're going to have to wait here with us until we sort out the situation," the agent said.

Chip looked over at Michael and Coach McDonald who were waiting and anxiously looking back at Chip. "You guys should probably go ahead. It looks like this could take a while."

To his surprise, both Michael and the coach started walking back toward him rather than heading into the stadium. "We're all part of the same team," Michael said to Chip. "We're not going anywhere without you."

It was almost an hour later before the security agents let them into the stadium. There were numerous people who examined Chip's security pass to make sure it wasn't a forgery and both Michael and the coach had to confirm Chip's identity. Chip was glad they had stayed behind because he wasn't sure he would have been allowed into the stadium without their help. He was also glad that they had all decided to head to the stadium early, as the delay might have otherwise caused them to miss their event.

* * *

Brian and Eric sat in the huge Estádio Olímpico João Havelange along with 60,000 other patrons. They were oblivious to the ordeal that Chip was going through at security as they watched the events that were already underway in the stadium. They both had binoculars so they could focus in on particular events and Eric had purchased a small radio so he could listen to the broadcast of the events through his earbuds. But they were focused on only one event right now, the Olympic 10,000 metre event which would be starting shortly.

Down on the track, Chip felt like his heart was going to burst right out of his chest. The anxiety of getting through security had now been replaced by the anxiety he felt knowing he was about to compete in his first Olympic event. He glanced at the twenty-eight other athletes competing in this event and wondered whether they were feeling any of the same emotions that he was. The Ethiopians looked completely calm, as if they were preparing for a summer stroll through the park. The Kenyans looked the same. The only one who looked as nervous as he did was the runner from Great Britain. He had won the gold medal at the London Olympics, gaining energy from the hometown crowd, and Chip could tell he felt the pressure to deliver one more time.

"Remember, no one is going to live or die depending on how you do in this race," Michael said to Chip as he shook his hand and pulled him in for a brief hug. He had obviously noticed the panic in Chip's eyes.

"Did you feel like this in your first Olympics?" Chip whispered to him.

"Absolutely," Michael said. "Just control the energy and use it to your advantage."

Chip took a deep breath and tried to tune out his surroundings and focus on controlling his breathing. He admired Michael for being so calm. He knew there was also immense pressure on Michael because these would be his last Olympics.

Due to the size of the field, there would be two starting rows for the event. Runners in the forward row, which included Michael, were required to stay in the outside lanes for the first half-lap. Chip was in the second row of competitors and they started on the inside lanes.

Up in the stands, Brian focused his binoculars on his son. Ironically, Chip stood beside the runner from Canada at the starting line and Brian couldn't help wishing his son had the red maple leaf on his jersey as well.

When the gun sounded the start of the race, Chip felt himself being jostled as the runners jockeyed for position. Since the race had twenty-five laps, Chip decided to hang back a bit at the start. The last thing he needed was to accidently get tripped and go down. When the two groups of runners merged, Chip found himself second last. He glanced over his shoulder and saw the runner from Great Britain behind him, as he always preferred to trail the field at the start. After the first five laps, Chip found himself in a nice rhythm and feeling quite comfortable.

"The pace is extremely slow," Eric said to his father up in the stands. He was listening to the broadcast of the race through his earbuds. "The broadcasters are saying they are running at a pedestrian pace which will favour the competitors with the best finishing kick."

"Well, Chip normally has a very strong finish," Brian said hopefully. However, he was concerned that Chip was too far from the front. The thought had barely crossed his mind when the runner from Great Britain made a move from the back and Chip followed him, gradually moving up to the middle of the pack. The entire field was now bunched again.

Over the next few laps, the sequence repeated itself. One of the runners would attempt to separate himself from the field, but would eventually fall back to the pack. First, it was one of the Ethiopians, then it was one of the Kenyans.

"The announcers are now saying they think the race will come down to the final 1,500 metres," Eric said to his father.

Suddenly there was a roar from the crowd as the Brazilian runner took over the lead and was trying to pull away from the field, spurred on by the cheering hometown crowd. The Ethiopians and two of the Kenyans quickly followed suit and Michael joined the breakaway group. Chip debated whether to go with them, but decided to stay just off the left shoulder of the British runner on the inside lane.

With the Brazilian leading the race, the crowd was now roaring and Eric couldn't hear anything through his earbuds, so he took them off and put them in his pocket.

With about two and a half laps remaining, the British runner decided to make a push and reel back the front-runners who were now about ten metres ahead of the main pack. Chip tried to go with him but found himself boxed in. Several other runners were now making a push as well so there was hardly any room to maneuver. By the time Chip could free himself from the pack, he was over a dozen metres behind the leader. He was now into a full-scale sprint and was gaining ground on the lead group, but he had fallen too far behind to make up the gap.

Up ahead, Michael found himself near the front with the Brazilian, the Kenyan and the two Ethiopian runners. As they entered the bell lap, the Brazilian was starting to weave from side to side as he was clearly out of gas. Michael still had lots of energy, but did he have the speed? The answer became apparent quickly as the other three runners pulled away from him down the stretch. To make it even worse, the British runner also overtook Michael in the last few steps before the finish line.

The results displayed on the huge screen in the stadium. Michael had finished fifth and Chip had finished ninth. Up in the stands, Eric and Brian were ecstatic with how well Chip had done. Chip had recorded his personal best time and had beaten several runners who had been ranked higher than him in the world rankings. But down on the track, Chip was disappointed in his performance. Actually, he could hardly control his anger. He had blown his chance at a medal by letting himself get boxed in. If he had been part of that lead group, he knew he could have matched them stride for stride down to the finish line.

Chip was congratulating the other runners when he saw Michael standing by himself with his head down. "Great race," Chip said, throwing his arm around Michael's shoulder.

Michael looked utterly dejected. "I was right there, but I just don't have the speed to finish anymore. I think I'm done. It's over."

"We've still got the 5,000 metre event," Chip said, but his words were falling on deaf ears.

*** CHAPTER 9 ***

That evening Maria headed back to the Copacabana to work at the bar. As she walked by the pool area, she saw the Girard family she had served at breakfast.

"Daddy, Daddy, come watch how well I can swim," the little girl yelled.

Mr. Girard was holding his young son in his arms so he passed his son to his wife, gave her a kiss and headed off to play with his daughter. "Okay, let's race to the other side of the pool," he said. The little girl swam as hard as she could with her father half a stride behind.

"Beat you," she giggled when she touched the other side.

"Yes you did," her father said. "You're probably fast enough to be in the Olympics."

Maria stared longingly at the happy family and wished her childhood had been so carefree. She hoped to meet a rich man someday and have a family of her own. Actually, he didn't have to be rich, just rich enough so she didn't have to live in the favela with her mother.

Maria headed into the bar and said hello to Eduardo, the bartender. "You're looking especially lovely tonight,"

Eduardo said. She knew Eduardo had a crush on her. He had always treated her well and she liked him well enough, but she was looking for more than he could offer.

"It looks like it's going to be a busy night," Maria said as she saw more and more tourists heading into the bar after their day watching the Olympics. As the night wore on, Maria received more than her fair share of tips. She also received numerous marriage proposals, with the frequency increasing the more the patrons drank.

When she was serving drinks to a large group of men, she flinched when she felt one of the men slide his hand under her dress and grab her ass. One of the other men at the table intervened on her behalf.

"Hey Dieter," the man said to his friend. "I don't think she needs a hand serving drinks."

"It's okay, I got this," Maria said as she calmly took the man's hand off of her ass. Dieter fell to his knees on the floor in pain as she calmly bent one of his fingers back, almost to the point of breaking it. "Now Dieter, I'm only going to warn you once. If I feel your hand on my ass again, you'll never be able to use this hand again. Got it?"

"Got it," Dieter gasped as she released his finger.

"I'm sorry for my friend's behavior," the stranger said. "But it probably wouldn't have happened if you hid those out of sight," he said glancing downward at her breasts. Maria had more than a few buttons undone on her dress. Showing a little, or a lot of cleavage certainly helped getting tips.

"Thanks for your concern," Maria said sternly, "but I don't tell you how to make a living so you have no right to tell me how I should make mine." They glared at each other for what seemed like an eternity, until he finally backed down.

As Maria was leaving the hotel bar after work that night,

she stopped in her tracks when she saw the same man waiting for her just outside the hotel. He approached when he saw her.

"I'd just like to apologize again for my friend's behavior this evening," he said, "and also for my comments about how you dress. I shouldn't have judged you so quickly."

"Apology accepted," Maria said, but she was still keeping her distance from him trying to assess the situation.

"I'm Greg," he said. "Greg Schneider." He extended his arm to shake her hand.

"I'm Maria," she answered, still keeping her distance. She didn't give her last name.

"I'm from Germany," Greg said. "We're part of a large group that came over to see the Olympics. I guess we had a little too much to drink tonight."

Maria didn't respond. She was starting to warm up a bit to this stranger, but was still a little guarded.

"It's pretty late for you to be out walking alone," Greg said, "and I hear some of the neighbourhoods around here can be a bit dangerous. Can I walk you home to make sure you get there safe and sound?"

"Oh, that's not necessary," Maria said. "I walk home by myself all the time. I'm probably safer walking through some of these parts than you are. But thank you for your concern."

"We don't get to see much of the city," Greg said, trying to keep the conversation going. "Our tour bus just takes us directly from the hotel to the Olympic venues and then straight back to the hotel."

"Well, if you're interested, I know the hotel offers tours of the city and a little bit of the outlying countryside."

"I might take one of those tours," Greg said. "Any chance you could join me and be my tour guide?"

"Oh, that's not necessary," Maria said. "The tours

offered by the hotel come with their own tour guide. They include a fancy lunch and dinner. They're pretty expensive."

"It will be my treat," Greg said.

"Oh, I don't think so," Maria said. She had been offered many such trips by men before and didn't want to feel obligated to them in any fashion. "But thank you anyway." She could see the disappointment on Greg's face immediately. "I should be heading home, or my mother will be worried." She was lying as she knew her mother wouldn't be worried at all, but Greg didn't know that.

"Well then, I shouldn't keep you any longer. Perhaps we'll run into each other again before I leave your beautiful country."

"Perhaps," Maria said as she turned and headed down the deserted street. As Maria walked through the favela on her way home, she found herself fantasizing about going on the tour with Greg. When she got home, her mother wasn't there. She rarely was. Maria placed the money that she had earned that night on the table. As she crawled into bed, she found herself dreaming about the life she wanted.

* * *

Brian and Eric stood about three rows back along the fourteenth fairway as the top American golfer went by. They could only get glimpses of him as they peered between the heads of the fans in front of them. Golf was back in the Olympics again and Brian was glad to see it.

"Did you know that Canada is the defending Olympic champion in golf?" Brian asked Eric.

"You're kidding," Eric said. "I just assumed it would be someone from the United States."

"Nope, George Lyon won the gold medal for Canada back in 1904, the last time golf was an Olympic event."

"Never heard of him," Eric said.

"Neither had I until I was reading about it. Back then it was a match-play event and he beat an American in the finals. This time it's a stroke-play event."

The American golfer was heavily favoured to add an Olympic gold medal to his already impressive list of wins. After he hit his shot, the massive crowd moved forward to follow him, allowing Brian and Eric to move up to the ropes alongside the fairway. One of the Canadian golfers was in the next group and he didn't have near the same following as the American golfers. As the next group approached, Brian and Eric noticed more and more red shirts and Canadian maple leaf pins. There were also quite a few fans wearing green and white, the colours of the Saskatchewan Roughriders.

"I wish your mother was alive to see this," Brian said. His wife had been born in Saskatchewan and the colours of the Roughriders would appear anywhere in the world whenever someone from that province was in competition. "I'm sure she'd be proud to see someone from Saskatchewan with a good chance of winning a medal in the Olympics. There's been a lot of guys who've won a gold medal in winter sports like hockey, but a gold medal in golf would be an unexpected bonus."

Eric remembered how passionate his mother had been about Saskatchewan. "Do you think Mom accomplished all of her goals in life before she passed away?" Eric was hoping his father would throw him another clue about their legacy.

"I don't think anyone ever accomplishes all of their goals," Brian said. He thought briefly before continuing. "I think she accomplished the most important ones. She set aside some money to help you and your brother with your education. You've now graduated and Chip should get his degree from Ohio State next year. She loved to travel, so I'm sure she would have wanted to see a bit more of the world, but she did get to see Australia and I know that was on her bucket list."

Brian and Eric followed the bearded golfer from Saskatchewan for the rest of his round and were pleased to see that he was in contention to win a medal. "What's with all of the guys sporting beards?" Eric asked when he noticed several of his fans in the crowd with them as well.

Brian chuckled. "I think that started a few years ago in the Fedex Cup. You know how hockey players grow beards during the NHL playoffs, right? Well since the Fedex Cup is sort of like the playoffs for golf, he started growing a beard and it sort of took off from there."

When they reached the last hole, the crowd surrounding the green was enormous, too large for Brian and Eric to get anywhere close to it. The Canadian had missed a few makeable putts over the last few holes, but so had many of the other competitors. This was the Olympics, not the typical PGA event, and the pressure was affecting them all.

Unfortunately, the Canadian had hit his approach shot into the bunker beside the green and would have to get up-and-down to have any shot at a medal. "Just hit it close," Brian whispered to himself as he watched.

The crowd stood up as he hit the shot so Brian couldn't even see the result. But the roar of the crowd left no doubt as to what had happened. It had gone in. Canada had won a medal in golf.

*** CHAPTER 10 ***

The next day, Brian and Eric headed off to the Olympic pool to see some of the swimming events. Canada wasn't really expected to be in contention for a medal in any of the these events, but it was an event that Eric wanted to see anyway.

Their seats were situated just behind a large contingent of fans from Australia. The Australians had a lot of potential medal winners on their team and their fans were being particularly boisterous about making sure everyone in the building knew that fact. It seemed a lot of the races came down to the final few strokes to decide whether an Australian or an American would win the gold medal. Sure enough, the women's 4x100 freestyle relay came right down to the finish and it was too close to determine who had won. When the results flashed on the screen showing Australia had won the gold medal, the Australian fans sitting in front of Brian and Eric rose from their seats and started singing.

"Ausie, Ausie, Ausie," yelled one of the fans leading the cheer.

"Oi, Oi, Oi," yelled the rest of the fans in response.

"Ausie, Ausie, Ausie – Oi, Oi, Oi," they repeated.

"Ausie, Oi – Ausie, Oi".

"Ausie, Ausie, Ausie – Oi, Oi, Oi".

The crowd broke into applause when the Australian fans were shown on the big-screen.

"I don't think we're going to be able to watch any more swimming events today," Brian said as he looked at his watch. "We've got to get going if we're going to make it to the stadium in time to watch Chip's heat in the 5,000 metres." Eric was hoping to be able to stay to see the men's 4x100 medley relay event, but agreed that it would be cutting things too close.

Sure enough, it took them longer than expected to make it to the Olympic track and they were still scurrying to their seats when the gun fired to signal the start of the first heat of the Olympic 5,000 metre event. Since Chip was going to be racing in the second heat, they still had about forty-five minutes until his race.

As they watched the first heat, they could see many of the same competitors that they had seen in the 10,000 metre event. The leaders consisted of Michael Porter from the U.S., two of the Ethiopian runners and one of the competitors from Kenya, with the rest of the runners grouped in a pack about ten metres behind. As the bell rang for the final lap, the race turned into a sprint to the finish line. And once again, Michael couldn't match the speed of the other runners down the stretch.

"Their times don't look that fast," Eric said. The top five finishers in each heat automatically qualified for the finals, plus the next best five times from either heat.

"Hopefully Chip can finish in the top five, so he doesn't have to worry about the times," Brian said.

When the next heat started, Chip immediately placed

himself as part of the lead group. The main pack of runners was about five metres back with, as usual, the runner from Great Britain trailing the field. "I hope Chip's not starting out too fast," Brian said. "He doesn't want to burn himself out early in the race."

"He probably doesn't want to get boxed in like he did in the last race," Eric said.

That's exactly what Chip was thinking down on the track. He was currently in second place, just off the right shoulder of the Kenyan runner who was in the lead. He had decided before the race he was going to follow whoever took the lead at any point in the race. Sure enough, the Brazilian runner tried to break away from the lead group and Chip stayed half a step behind him. With two laps remaining, Chip could feel his lungs and his legs starting to burn. He had been determined not to leave anything in the tank for this race, but he was starting to feel like he was running on fumes at this point. When they started the final sprint in the last five hundred metres, Chip realized he was in trouble as he had nothing left to give. Neither did the Brazilian runner. The first to pass them was the runner from Great Britain but a few more passed by the time they reached the finish line. Chip looked up at the big screen and saw that he had finished eighth in his heat.

"Did he make it?" Eric asked his dad.

"I'm not sure," Brian said. "It seemed like their times were faster than the first heat, but I don't know."

They held their breath waiting for the results to be displayed indicating who had qualified for the finals. It was only a few seconds but it seemed like an eternity until the qualifying list appeared on the screen. It showed a large "Q" beside the names of the first five runners in each heat and a small "q" beside the names of the next best five times. They were relieved to see a small "q" beside Chip's name meaning he had qualified for the finals. There was a loud roar from the crowd when they saw that the Brazilian runner had also made it through.

Down on the track, Chip was relieved to see that he had qualified for the finals, but he was also angry with himself for his strategy during the race. When he went into the change room, he was surprised to see Michael still there. "Did you make it?" Michael asked him.

"Barely," Chip answered. "I didn't run a very smart race." Chip already knew that Michael had qualified for the final as he had finished fourth in his heat.

"I can't match their speed down the stretch," Michael said, "and the pace in our heat was pretty slow. I don't know how I'm going to beat them in the final."

* * *

Two days later Chip and Michael were back at the small track used for training preparing for the finals to be held the next day. "Coach McDonald said he wants to talk to you," Michael said as they were doing their stretches.

The coach was sitting on a bench by himself, well away from any of the competitors. "How are you feeling?" the coach asked when Chip sat down beside him.

"Pretty good," Chip said, but he was lying. Battling Crohn's was taking more and more of a toll on Chip and he'd been up several times during the night to go to the bathroom. It seemed like he'd spent half of his life in the bathroom lately.

"I want to talk to you about strategy in the finals," the coach said.

"I know I went out too fast in the last race," Chip said, "but I didn't want to get boxed in like I did in the 10,000 metre event. I'll run a smarter race in the finals."

"Actually, I was wondering if you'd consider pushing the

pace even more."

"I don't understand. Why?"

The coach paused before answering. "This will be Michael's last Olympics and we think he has a good chance of winning the gold medal. But he can't match the speed of the other runners down the stretch so we need someone to push the pace so it becomes more of an endurance race rather than a sprint to the finish line."

Chip looked confused, but then he realized what his coach was asking him. "So you want me to be the one to push the pace."

"The Ethiopians run as a team," the coach said. "So do the Kenyans. We have to think like a team as well."

Chip didn't respond. He knew he only had an outside chance of winning a medal himself, but that goal had been driving him for years. He wasn't sure he wanted to abandon that goal now.

"Michael won a bronze in his first Olympics," the coach said, "and a silver in his second. If he could win medals in three straight Olympics and top it off with a gold medal, it would become his legacy."

Chip still didn't respond.

"The choice is up to you," the coach said. "Just do what you think is best."

Chip headed back over to the track to run some wind sprints and Michael headed over to talk to him. "Don't do it," Michael said. He knew what the coach had asked him to do. "Don't sacrifice your own chances at a medal just to help me win one. If I can't do it on my own, then I don't deserve it."

Chip had no idea what he was going to do.

*** CHAPTER 11 ***

As Maria headed into work that night, she was surprised to see Greg sitting at the bar. "Good evening," he said to Maria. "I was hoping to run into you here tonight. Perhaps we could get a drink together later after your shift ends."

"I'm not sure that's possible," Maria replied, "as I work right up until closing and Eduardo here is a very strict boss." She gave Eduardo a quick wink as she said it.

But Greg ignored the brush-off. "Bartender, I'll have another," he said raising his glass to Eduardo.

Maria was kept hopping keeping up with the large number of customers that night, but Greg spoke to her every time she came back to the bar to have Eduardo fill her drink order. Greg was quite witty and funny and Maria was starting to warm up to him. He was tall and blonde. Maria found herself wondering what their kids would look like.

"Just say the word," Eduardo whispered to Maria while filling one of her orders, "and I'll throw his ass out of here."

"Oh, he's harmless and not so bad," Maria replied.

"I don't like him," Eduardo said. "Not one little bit."

Eduardo saw guys trying to pick up Maria every night at the bar and although he didn't like it, he had sort of grown used to it. But there was something about Greg that rubbed him entirely the wrong way.

"You know, I signed up for one of those tours that you mentioned," Greg said to Maria later on that night. "It would be great if you could join me."

"I'll think about it," Maria said smiling.

"Hey, I'm making progress," Greg announced to the rest of the patrons at the bar. "I've gone from an *out-and-out no* to an *I'll think about it*. Bartender, I think my work here for the night is done." He threw a wad of cash on the bar. "Keep the change."

Maria and Eduardo watched him walk out of the bar. "I still don't like that guy," Eduardo said with a scowl.

As Maria walked home from the bar that night, she found herself thinking about Greg and the idea of going on the tour with him. When she walked into her place, she found her mother sitting at the kitchen table with two strange men. The two men looked like they had crawled out from under a rock somewhere. Her mother was tending to a wound on the shoulder of one of the men.

"What's going on here?" Maria asked her mother.

"This is none of your concern," her mother replied. "How much money did you make tonight?"

Maria threw the money on the kitchen table in front of her mother. She looked at the man who was getting his arm tended to by her mother and saw the bullet that had been removed from his shoulder lying on the table. The bullet lay in a small pool of blood.

Maria turned with disgust and headed off to her room. This was not the first time she had seen her mother remove a bullet from someone. As she lay in bed that night, Maria decided she was going to find a way to join Greg on the tour. She had to do something to get out of here.

* * *

The next day Brian and Eric found themselves almost as excited as the runners as each competitor was introduced before the start of the Olympic 5,000 metre final. There was a huge cheer when Chip was introduced and his picture appeared on the big screen in the stadium. The Brazilian runner was the last to be introduced, so the crowd was in a frenzy before the starting gun even sounded.

"What strategy do you think Chip will be using in the finals?" Eric asked his father.

"I have no idea," Brian replied. They had not spoken to Chip since the start of the Olympics. However, Chip had posted an update on his Facebook page indicating that he'd have to come up with a better strategy in the finals to have any chance at a medal.

As Chip stood on the starting line waiting for the race to begin, he still hadn't made up his own mind about what he was going to do. When the starting gun sounded, the Brazilian runner immediately jumped into the lead which got the home-town crowd into even more of a frenzy. Chip decided to follow his lead. As they finished the first lap, Chip looked up to see the huge screen in the stadium and could see they were about five metres ahead of the pack. The screen displayed their lap time which indicated they were on pace to set a new Olympic record.

The positioning after the fourth lap was pretty much the same, but Chip could tell that the Brazilian runner was starting to slow down. The initial adrenaline rush the hometown crowd had provided him was starting to wane. Chip decided to take the lead and keep pushing the pace. At first, the Brazilian runner kept up with him but dropped back to the main pack after another lap.

As he looked at the big screen as he completed the seventh lap, Chip could see that his lead had grown to over ten metres and he was now two seconds under the Olympic record pace.

"He's going out way too fast," Eric said to his father.

"He must have a plan," Brian replied, but even he wondered what Chip was doing.

After eight laps, Chip's lead was fifteen metres and the field was spread out in a line behind him, with the last runner almost half a lap behind. Almost in unison, the two Ethiopian runners and the two Kenyan runners decided that they couldn't let Chip get too far ahead so they picked up their pace to try to reel him in. Michael Porter joined the group in pursuit.

Chip looked up at the big screen as he completed the ninth lap and could see what was happening behind him. But he refused to back off the incredible pace he had set so far. In fact, he increased it even more so that he was now almost four seconds under the Olympic record pace.

When he completed the tenth lap, he looked up at the big screen again, but his vision had become so blurry that he couldn't really see what was going on anymore. But he knew they were coming up behind him. "Only two and a half laps to go," he thought to himself. "Just keep pushing."

He turned his focus to just the few feet of track in front of him on every stride. Hi lungs were screaming and his legs were burning. And oh, the pain in his gut. He was sure his guts were going to come streaming out of his body at any second. But he continued to push.

Chip could tell by the roar of the crowd that the runners behind him were getting closer and closer. He could now hear their footsteps. Or could he? He didn't really trust any of his senses anymore. His vision was just a blurry kaleidoscope of colours and his hearing consisted of noise, just noise, with no distinct sound. He wasn't sure what was real anymore.

But then he heard it, the distinct sound of the bell signaling the final lap, and it seemed to pull him back into focus. He realized that someone was just about to pass him. Was it one of the Ethiopian runners, one of the runners from Kenya, or maybe that runner from Great Britain? Chip dug in even harder refusing to let him pass, but it was no use. He had nothing left.

It was only then that Chip realized it was Michael. "Finish it," Chip said as Michael went by him.

Chip wanted to fall down right there and then, but his body just kept taking stride after stride. He felt like one of those horses that keeps on running to the finish line, even after the jockey has fallen off. His body was now on auto-pilot, just doing what it had been trained to do for all of those years.

Chip didn't know how many more runners passed him before the finish line. His goal now was simply to finish, which he did. He had no idea what position he had finished in. He didn't even know if Michael had won the race. He was numb.

Chip staggered towards the infield and collapsed on the grass. Within a few seconds, one of the paramedics came rushing over and placed an oxygen mask on him. Someone else placed a cold cloth on his forehead. He knew people were talking to him but he couldn't really see them or understand what they were saying.

Up in the stands, Brian focused his binoculars trying to get a glimpse of his son, but he couldn't really see him with all of the paramedics and trainers hovering over him.

"Is he okay?" Eric asked.

"I don't know," Brian replied. "I can't see him."

The big screen in the stadium showed a brief shot of Chip trying to get up, but the paramedic held him down and told him to just lay there for a few more minutes. Then the screen displayed the results of the final and showed the winner taking his victory lap of the stadium.

Several minutes had elapsed since the end of the race, but Chip continued to lay on his back on the infield getting treatment from the paramedics. He was now starting to understand what the paramedics were asking him and could respond with somewhat coherent answers. His vision was also starting to regain focus rather than being just a blur of colours. Suddenly a shadow hovered over him with a huge cape, blocking out the light.

"Do you think you can get up?" It was Michael, draped in a huge American flag. Michael reached down, grabbed Chip's hand and then gradually pulled him to his feet, with the paramedics helping to make sure that Chip wasn't going to collapse again.

"I owe you one," Michael said as they walked off the track together, arm in arm. "I couldn't have won the gold without you."

*** CHAPTER 12 ***

Two days later, Brian and Eric waited for Chip in the lobby of the Sheraton. Brian was planning to fly back home later that morning, but Eric and Chip were planning to stay for a few more days to tour Rio de Janeiro and a bit of Brazil. Chip was leaving the high security environment at the Olympic Village and taking his father's spot at the hotel, where he could be a typical tourist.

"Do you think Chip will be disappointed with his tenth place finish?" Eric asked his father.

"He shouldn't be," Brian answered. "He was ranked twelfth in the world coming into the Olympics and he finished ninth in the 10,000 metres and tenth in the 5,000 metres."

"I was hoping he could have held on for a medal in that last race," Eric said.

Brian glanced at his watch. Chip was now over half an hour late and he was getting concerned that he wouldn't get much time to visit with him before he had to leave to catch his flight. Finally, he saw Chip coming through the revolving doors of the hotel. "Congratulations son," Brian said as he rushed over to give Chip a huge bear hug. "I'm so proud of you."

"Thanks Dad," Chip said.

"Me too," Eric said, taking his turn to give his brother a hug. "For a while there, I thought you were going to set a new Olympic record time."

"I was pushing the pace as much as I could," Chip said, "but I didn't have enough left at the end to finish it. Fortunately, Michael did." Chip waved to Michael who was hovering in the background. "Michael, this is my father, Brian, and my brother, Eric. This is Michael Porter, Olympic gold medalist."

"Nice to meet you," Michael said. "I don't think I could have done it without Chip's help."

"Eric, I hope you don't mind," Chip said, "but I asked Michael to join us on the tour. He doesn't fly back to the states until tomorrow and wanted to get out of the Olympic Village and away from the media for a while."

They all visited in the lobby for the next hour, with Chip and Michael telling them the inside story of what it's like to be in the Olympics. Brian could tell by the stories that Chip told that his Olympic experience had been a positive one, even though he hadn't won a medal. They were interrupted in their stories when the shuttle-bus driver announced that the next shuttle bus was now leaving for the airport.

"That's my cue," Brian said. "My flight leaves in a little over three hours and it will take a while to get through security at the airport." He rose and gave both his sons another hug before he departed. "See you back home in a week," he said as he boarded the airport shuttle.

It was about forty five minutes later when a luxury coach pulled up in front of the hotel. The tour that Eric, Chip and Michael had signed up for was a first-class tour that was only offered to the wealthiest of clients. Brian had paid for his two sons to join the tour. Michael had charged it to his credit card. "This tour isn't cheap. If my agent doesn't come through with some big endorsement deal, I'll be hocking this thing to pay for it." Michael clutched the gold medal that was hanging around his neck, but carefully hidden from view underneath his shirt. He hadn't taken the medal off since they had put it around his neck, not even when he showered.

The tour included champagne and hors d'oeuvres served to the patrons before the tour started, a comprehensive tour of the sites of Rio, a fancy lunch, a tour of some of the outlying countryside of Brazil, and a full course dinner at the end of the tour. When the three of them boarded the luxury coach, there were only six or seven people taking part in the tour, including them.

"Good morning," said the hostess after they had boarded. "We'll be making a couple more stops to pick up guests at other hotels before we begin the tour, but we should be ready to get started shortly. In the meantime, please let me know if there is anything you need."

The tour bus headed to the Marriott where a few more people boarded the bus. Eric could easily tell that two of them were from Australia as their accents were pretty thick. He thought he recognized them as part of the Australian fans from the swimming events they had watched. There was also an older couple who joined the tour along with a couple of teenagers. At first, Eric thought they were together but they sat in different parts of the coach. The bus was still less than half full as it headed to the Copacabana to pick up more passengers.

At the Copacabana, Maria was attempting to use all of her charms on the manager to convince him to let her join the tour. "Not a chance," the manager said. "It costs a lot of money to take this tour. I can't let you go for free."

"I'll make it up to you," Maria said giving him a coy smile.

"That's not going to work with me," the manager said. He was well aware of Maria's reputation of flirting to get what she wanted.

Maria looked inside the lobby and could see the wealthy guests drinking champagne and eating hors d'oeuvres. She could see Greg inside with all of the other guests. He had offered to pay for her to join the tour, but she had politely declined. However, she was still hoping to be able to find a way onto the tour bus.

"Hello Maria," a lady said as she tapped her on the shoulder. Maria turned to see that it was Sylvia and Jean-Pierre Girard, the couple she had served at breakfast a few days earlier. "Are you going to be working on this tour?" Sylvia asked.

Maria paused before answering. "I'm not sure."

"We're quite looking forward to it," Sylvia said. "We arranged for a sitter for the kids and it will be the first thing we've done on this trip with just the two of us." She hugged her husband's arm as she said it.

Just then, the tour bus pulled up in front of the Copacabana and the guests started getting ready to board. Maria moved back behind one of the pillars of the hotel as she didn't want Greg to see her.

"Boy, I sure hope she's part of this tour," Chip said as he looked at Maria through the bus window.

"Down boy," Eric said when he saw her. "If she's that attractive and rich enough to be part of this tour, she's probably already spoken for."

Greg took his seat on the bus. He had been watching for Maria, hoping that she would be joining him for the tour, but it appeared that she was going to stand him up.

"Good morning Mr. and Mrs. Taylor," the Manager said

to the next two people to board the tour bus. The manager ticked their names off of his list and did the same for the four Japanese men who boarded after them.

After the last passenger had boarded the bus and the manager had ticked off all of the names, he nodded to the driver and started to head back into the hotel. Maria saw her chance and stepped out from behind the pillar. "Sorry I'm late," she said as she boarded the bus and gave the driver her best smile.

The driver was just about to question whether she was authorized to be on the tour when he heard Greg call her name from a few rows back in the bus. "Maria, back here." The driver decided not to question her. She was obviously one of the guests.

Maria made her way back and sat down beside Greg. "I'm so glad you could join me on the tour," Greg said. "I know that it's really expensive. Are you sure you don't want it to be my treat?"

"No, that's not necessary," Maria said. "I got the staff discount."

Eric and Chip had watched Maria board the bus and sit down beside Greg. "See, I told you she was taken," Eric said to his brother. But even Eric was disappointed to see that she had a boyfriend.

There were now about twenty passengers on board for the tour and for the next few hours the bus took them to the various sites in Rio. They travelled to the statue of Christ the Redeemer on top of Corcovado Mountain.

"Dad and I saw this statue the day we flew in," Eric said. "It seems even bigger from down here on the ground."

They were treated to a seafood lunch after they rode a cable-car to the top of Sugar Loaf Mountain. "I'm supposed to be on a restricted diet and not eat too much seafood," Eric said, "but this is so delicious." He went back up for a second helping and ended up standing behind the two Australians in line at the buffet.

"Hi, I'm Eric Baxter," he said while waiting his turn in line. "I think I saw you guys over at the Olympic pool a few days ago. How did Australia end up in the relays?"

"G'day," the first Australian said. "I'm Lucas Williams and this is my brother Oliver." His brother nodded hello, but was concentrating on filling his plate with seafood. "We won a few gold medals in the individual races and one of the women's relay races, but only got a bronze in the men's 4x100 freestyle relay and a silver in the medley relay. Damn Americans beat us out at the end in both races." He suddenly realized he might be talking to an American. "Sorry, are you American?"

"No, I'm Canadian," Eric said pointing to show them a red maple leaf logo on the sleeve of his shirt. "But, be careful because my brother ran for the American team even though he was born in Canada." Eric pointed to where Chip was sitting. "And the fellow sitting next to him won a gold medal for the U.S." Eric invited the Australians to join them at their table.

"Guys, this is Lucas and Oliver Williams from Australia. This is my brother Chip and this is Michael Porter. Michael won the gold medal in the 5,000 metre event."

"Congrats mate," Lucas said.

"Thanks," Michael said as he pulled out the gold medal from underneath his shirt to show it to the Australians. "But I couldn't have done it without help from Chip who set a hell of a pace." Michael reached over with his right arm and gave Chip a gentle push on his shoulder.

Over at another table, Maria and Greg were enjoying the extravagant meal. "So what do you do for a living back in Germany," Maria asked.

"I'm in politics," Greg said. "I'm the policy advisor for

the CDU party."

Maria was disappointed to hear that he was a politician. She didn't know what politicians were like in Germany but she didn't think much of the ones they had in Brazil. There were constant reports of corruption at every level of government and there had been numerous protests by the Brazilian people over the last few years leading up to the Olympic games. Maria had even participated in a few protests herself, but she wasn't sure they did any good. Whenever they got rid of one corrupt politician, he seemed to be replaced by another just as corrupt. "Oh well," Maria thought to herself. "That's only one strike against him. Nobody's perfect."

"Hello Maria," Sylvia Girard said as she looked for an open table along with her husband. "Do you mind if we join you?" she asked as they approached.

"Please do," Maria said. "This is Greg Schneider. He's a guest at the hotel visiting from Germany. Greg, this is Jean-Pierre and Sylvia Girard. They're from the United States."

Another couple who were looking for a place to sit overheard the conversation and decided to sit at their table as well. "Did I hear someone say they're from Germany?" the man said. "We're from Germany as well. I'm Klaus Weber and this is my wife Anja."

Before long, the Girards were talking about their kids and showing pictures of them to everyone at the table. Maria could hear the love in their voices as they spoke about their kids and she envied them immensely. The Webers were an older couple and responded by pulling out pictures of their grandchildren, which they also showed with great pride.

"If I hear one more person talking about their kids, I think I'll shoot myself," Greg leaned in and whispered to Maria. "Let's get out of here."

"Strike two," Maria thought to herself. She could never be with a man who didn't like kids. But she just smiled at him and politely excused herself as they left the table. "I think the tour bus is going to be leaving shortly," Maria said to the Girards and the Webers as they headed off.

After the extravagant lunch, the bus did a brief tour of one of the favelas. It wasn't just any favela, it was the one that Maria called home, although she didn't disclose that fact to Greg. "I can't believe some people have to live in these shacks," Greg said to Maria when he saw them. "I thought they were going to try to get rid of all of the slum areas in Rio by the time the Olympics started. I've heard they're filled with thieves and drug dealers. It would probably be best if they just blew the whole place up."

"Strike three," Maria thought to herself. The more she was getting to know Greg, the more she was starting to realize he wasn't going to be her Prince Charming. She couldn't hold it in any longer. "You know there are real people who live there and you can't just blow up their homes, even if they are shacks," Maria said. "Not everyone who lives there is a criminal. A lot of us work very, very hard and are doing the best we can."

"You're one of them?" Greg asked, suddenly seeming embarrassed to be seen with Maria. He glanced over his shoulder to see if any of the other patrons had been listening to their conversation, but everyone else seemed to be listening to the tour guide and looking out of the windows of the bus.

"Yes, I was born there," Maria said, fighting back tears. "Some people have nowhere else to go. They're trapped in their lives with no means to escape."

"I'm sorry," Greg said. "I would have never thought…," but he didn't finish his sentence. He didn't have to.

"We're about to leave the city," the tour guide said as they began the second half of the tour. "We'll be heading to one of the rainforests of Brazil where you'll be able to see monkeys, toucans and many other birds and animals that are native to this area."

The bus drove for about twenty minutes out into the Brazilian countryside. Greg and Maria didn't say a word to each other. Maria just looked out the window of the bus. Greg looked like he wanted to be anywhere else than where he was.

Several rows back, Eric and Chip were also looking out of the window, amazed at how quickly the landscape was changing. Only half an hour ago, they were in the middle of a large city and now they felt they were out in the middle of nowhere.

The luxury bus had been travelling on one of the main highways but then turned off the highway and started heading down some dirt roads that were barely as wide as the bus. The driver was surprised when the road he had planned to take had a roadblock on it, with signs pointing the way to an alternate route. "Don't be alarmed," the tour guide announced to the people on the bus. "Our driver knows all of the back roads into the rainforest."

The bus picked up speed as it headed down a steep hill. As it neared the bottom of the hill, it was suddenly rammed on the side by a truck that came flying out of a small trail hidden by trees. Eric was thrown from his seat onto the floor with Chip tumbling on top of him.

"Are you okay?" Chip asked, pulling himself off of his brother and back into his seat.

"Yeah, I think so," Eric replied. "What the hell happened?"

Eric looked at the other passengers who had also been sent flying by the impact. He helped an older couple back into their seats. They appeared shaken, but didn't seem to be seriously hurt. There was a lot of shouting as the people on the bus dealt with the chaos that surrounded them. Suddenly, there was an eerie silence as everyone seemed to stop talking at the same time. When Eric looked out the bus window, he could see their bus was now surrounded by four military-style trucks. He looked toward the front of the bus and saw two men board the bus carrying weapons.

"Todos fora do ônibus!" yelled one of the gunmen.

The bus driver yelled something and one of the gunmen shot him without hesitation and then threw his body off the bus. "Pressa, pressa. Todos fora do ônibus!" the gunmen yelled again. They waved their guns directing everybody to get off of the bus. As they did so, each person had a black canvas bag shoved over their head and they were thrown into the back of one of the trucks.

"Chip, where are you?" Eric yelled. He never heard the answer as he was hit on the side of the head with the butt end of a rifle. He was only semi-conscious as he was tossed around in the back of the truck as it raced through the forest. He thought they drove for a while, but he really had no idea because everything seemed to be happening so fast.

Suddenly, the truck stopped and he was pulled from the truck and thrown to the ground. His hands were tied together with a long rope and as they pushed him forward, he realized he was tied to the same rope as the person in front of him. Then he felt someone pushed into him from behind and he realized there were several of them that had been tied together. It was like they were part of a chain-gang of prisoners.

"De Março, março rapidamente!" came the command as they were dragged forward.

They were led through the forest for what seemed like forever, tripping regularly over the underbrush. When one person would trip, it would trigger a chain reaction so that almost all of them would fall down. They would be dragged to their feet by the gunmen and pushed forward again.

Chip was going through a similar experience, although he was in a different group of prisoners than Eric. Chip could tell that Michael was the person behind him as they marched through the forest because he would land on him every time they fell.

"Just follow my lead," Chip said. "We'll get through this." He didn't get a response from Michael. He helped Michael to his feet several times after they had fallen. Chip could also tell that it was a woman in front of him in their group, but he had no idea who she was.

"Pare de andar!" came the yell as they moved into what seemed to be a clearing. They came to an abrupt stop as someone pulled on the rope sending them all tumbling to the ground. As he lay on the ground, Eric could feel the ropes around his hands being untied. He was dragged to his feet and pushed forward. When the hood over his head was removed, he saw three men with bandanas over their faces. They waved their rifles as they directed him to move forward toward a large canopy that was surrounded with barbed wire.

When Chip's group of prisoners were halted, Maria was the first to have her hood removed. "Don't try to fight them," Maria whispered to Chip. "They have guns and they will shoot you."

Chip's hood was removed next, followed by Michael's. Michael seemed completely disoriented and looked like he was going to fall down. As he swayed from side to side, he leaned into Chip who supported him with his shoulder to keep him on his feet.

When Greg's hood was removed, he panicked when he saw the masked men with their rifles. He started to make a run for it, not realizing that he was still tied to the rest of the prisoners in his group. As he started to run, he sent the rest of them flying to the ground. Chip let out a piercing yell as he dragged into the barbed wire fence, slicing his leg open in the process.

Although he couldn't see him, Eric recognized his brother's voice immediately. "Chip!" Eric yelled. Once again, he was hit across the side of the head with the butt end of a rifle. This time, he was knocked out cold.

*** CHAPTER 13 ***

"Are you okay?" Maria asked Eric as she cradled his head. "You were out for quite a while."

Eric tried to get up, but the pain and dizziness in his head quickly told him it was too soon for that. "Where's my brother?"

"I don't know," Maria said. "There's a bunch of us being held here, but I don't know which one is your brother."

Eric tried to get up again and this time he fought through the pain and dizziness until he was up on his feet. They were being held under what looked like a huge tent and it felt like it was about a thousand degrees under the tarp. There were bodies strewn everywhere, but Eric quickly focused in on his brother.

"Chip," he yelled as he staggered over to him. When he got to him, Eric could see that Chip was in even worse shape than he was. He was awake, but Eric could see a huge gash in his leg and he had lost a lot of blood.

"We need some water and a doctor!" Eric yelled as he headed toward one of the gunmen.

He was greeted with a rifle pointed straight at his head. "Pare ali mesmo ou eu vou filmar você!" yelled the gunman.

"He needs a doctor," Eric pleaded. Eric heard the rifle being cocked.

Maria grabbed Eric's arm and pulled him back from the gunman. "He's going to kill you if you don't back off."

"But I can't just let my brother die," Eric pleaded.

Maria slowly walked toward the guard. "Por favor, precisamos de alguma água para limpar sua ferida e precisamos de um médico ou outra coisa, ele vai morrer. Por favor."

The gunman stared at Maria, then turned to one of the other gunmen and yelled. "Dê-lhes um pouco de água."

A few minutes later, two of the guards appeared carrying a large bucket of water which they placed in the middle of the complex. Maria tore a strip off of the bottom of her dress, dipped it in the water and took it over to Eric who started to clean the huge gash in Chip's leg. Chip moaned every time Eric touched him, but it had to be done. After the wound had been cleaned, it looked a lot better but Eric was pretty sure it was infected.

Eric and Maria surveyed the rest of the prisoners. It felt like they were in a MASH unit, doing triage on wounded soldiers. When Maria saw Greg, she found him huddled on the ground almost in a fetal position. "Greg, are you okay?" she asked.

"Just leave me alone," Greg said as he turned away from her. "Are these guys friends of yours? Is that why you lured me onto the tour bus?" Maria didn't know how to respond.

"Maria," someone called from behind her. She turned to see that it was Sylvia Girard. "Can you help us?" she asked. Maria could see that Mr. Girard wasn't in very good shape at all. He was holding his arm as if he had a separated shoulder and he looked like he was in a lot of pain.

"I'm okay," he said bravely. "I guess I shouldn't have tried to fight them off, but they were hurting Sylvia." Sylvia was holding onto her husband for dear life.

"I'm sure we'll all be okay," Maria said to them. Mr. Girard smiled at Maria. He knew that Maria was just telling his wife what she wanted, maybe needed, to hear.

As Eric walked around the camp, he saw a German couple and the two guys from Australia that had been on the tour. They all had numerous cuts and bruises on them from their trek through the forest, but appeared to be in pretty good shape. He also saw four Japanese men huddled together. They were all removing their watches and other jewelry and burying them in a small hole they had dug in the ground. "These guys are interested in more than your jewelry," Eric thought to himself.

"Michael, are you alright?" Eric asked when he found Michael on the ground, leaning up against one of the poles that held up the tent. He didn't get a response. Eric knelt down beside him. He didn't have any obvious injuries, but his eyes were glazed over. Eric was pretty sure he was in shock.

"I think everyone who was on the tour bus is here, with the exception of the bus driver and the tour guide," Maria said to Eric. They had all seen the bus driver get shot, but had no idea what had happened to the tour guide. "Everybody here is injured and a few of them are in shock, but I think most will be okay." She paused before continuing. "Except for your brother."

"We've got to get him a doctor," Eric said as he started over toward the gunmen.

"Let me," Maria said, pulling him back.

She walked slowly toward the gunmen with her hands held up to her side. "Por quanto tempo você está indo para nos manter aqui?"

"Você vai ser lançado quando nós receber o nosso dinheiro!," replied one of the gunmen.

"Assim você não vai conseguir algum dinheiro para um homem morto," Maria said. "Ele precisa de um médico."

"I don't speak Spanish," Eric said when she returned. "What did they say?"

"It's not Spanish, it's Portuguese," Maria said. "I asked them when we would be released and they said we would be released when they get their money. They're obviously holding us for ransom. I told them they won't get any ransom money for a dead man and that your brother needs a doctor."

About two hours later, one of the guards arrived with a first aid kit and threw it in Maria's direction. It was a small plastic box that had the logo of the tour company on the top. The guard had obviously retrieved it from the tour bus. Maria opened the kit, but quickly realized it contained only basic materials. Still, it was better than nothing.

She found a small bottle of alcohol in the kit. "I'm going to need your help," Maria said to Eric. "This is going to hurt like hell so you're going to have to hold him still."

Chip was only half conscious, which was probably a good thing considering what she was about to do. She quickly poured the alcohol onto the open wound and Chip let out an enormous scream. Eric tried to hold his brother still and Maria held onto his wounded leg so he couldn't do any more damage to it. Chip passed out within a few seconds due to the pain.

Maria carefully wrapped Chip's leg in some gauze she found in the first aid kit, pulling it tightly to try to close the wound. "That's about all I can do," she said to Eric. "He really needs stitches."

Maria then went to the other prisoners and applied

whatever first aid she could. It wasn't very long until all of the supplies in the first aid kit were gone. She came back and sat beside Eric, who was standing vigil beside his brother. The rest of the prisoners were now sleeping. It was now almost completely dark which in some ways was a blessing because it reduced the temperature from being impossibly hot to just unbearably hot. The only light came from a camping lantern the guards had.

"Are you a nurse?" Eric whispered to Maria.

"No. I've been called a lot of things in my life, but never a nurse," Maria whispered back.

"Well you did a great job treating everyone's wounds. Where did you learn to do that?"

"You don't want to know."

"Well, you've obviously seen some medical procedures done before. Was your father or your mother a doctor?"

Maria laughed. She wasn't sure how much information to share with Eric. But then she thought she probably wasn't going to make it out of this situation alive anyway, so what the hell.

"I'm a fraud," Maria confessed. "I'm not rich like the rest of you or come from a rich family. I snuck onto the tour bus. I live in the favela, the one the tour bus drove by today. My father was a drug dealer and a gang leader, or was until he was killed. My mother now runs the business. I've seen my share of people stitched up after being stabbed or shot. People don't go to the hospital where I come from, the surgery takes place right on the kitchen table."

Eric didn't know how to respond. "Well you probably saved some lives here today," he finally said. "I know you saved mine. I'm pretty sure they would have shot me if you hadn't intervened."

"Yeah, well I wouldn't say I saved your life just yet. I may have just delayed the execution."

*** CHAPTER 14 ***

Brian had just boarded the airplane in Houston for the second leg of his journey back to Toronto. He was extremely tired as once again he had failed to get much sleep on the long overnight flight from Rio de Janeiro to Houston. To make matters worse, the Houston airport was bustling with activity and he hadn't found a quiet place to rest while waiting for the connecting flight. For some reason, he had an uneasy feeling that he couldn't seem to shake.

"Attention passengers," announced the stewardess from the front of the plane. "If passenger Brian Baxter is on board, could he kindly identify himself to one of the attendants by pressing the call button."

Brian gave a heavy sigh. "Great," he thought to himself, "they're going to tell me that they lost my luggage on the flight from Rio to Houston." He raised his hand and pressed the button and the stewardess smiled and came toward him.

"I'm so sorry, Mr. Baxter, but could you follow me to the front of the plane?" she asked politely.

"What's this about?" Brian asked.

"Just follow me," she said, "and we'll explain everything when we get to the front. Please bring your carry-on baggage."

Brian grabbed his carry-on bag from the overhead bin and followed her to the front. Several passengers looked at him suspiciously as he made his way up the aisle. He could tell they were wondering if he was some kind of a criminal who had just been caught trying to sneak out of the country.

When he reached the front of the plane, he found two men in suits waiting for him.

"Mr. Baxter, Mr. Brian Baxter?" one of the men asked.

"Yes, I'm Brian Baxter. What is this about?"

"There's been an incident. Please come with us and we'll explain."

Brian followed the two men down the passenger walkway from the plane back towards the terminal. When they reached the terminal, the two men steered Brian off to the side. "I'm Detective Gosling and this is Detective Westbrook. We're with the FBI. We've been advised that there has been an incident in Brazil concerning your sons. We've been asked to bring you to FBI headquarters in Houston so you can be apprised of all of the details."

Brian's heart stopped. "Have they been in an accident? Are they hurt?"

"I'm sorry sir," Detective Gosling said. "We don't know any of the details, but it will all be explained to you at FBI headquarters. Is this all of your luggage?" The detectives had already arranged to have his luggage pulled from the plane.

"Yes, I think so," Brian said. He could hardly catch his breath as he imagined all of the worst scenarios. The officers led Brian out of the airport terminal to where their car was waiting. The car quickly weaved its way through traffic and pulled into the basement parking garage of a large building. As soon as the car stopped, his car door was opened by another agent who escorted him into the elevator and up to the eighth floor. Brian was led into a large room with multiple big-screen TV monitors on the wall, several computers scattered on three large tables and a multitude of telephones.

"Mr. Baxter," said one of the men who was waiting in the room. "I'm Detective Steve Mitchell. I'm the lead agent on this case and this is Detective Ryan Johnson who is second in command. If you'll join the others, we'll explain the situation."

Detective Mitchell appeared to be middle-aged or older, based on the bald spot on the top of his head that looked like it had been there for several years. The stress of working for the FBI for over twenty years was shown by the worry lines around his eyes. Detective Johnson was quite a bit younger and his baby-faced complexion indicated he was relatively new to this line of work.

Brian sat down at one of the tables and saw several other people sitting at the tables around the room. One of the ladies at the next table was crying and her husband was trying to console her. The others just looked in shock.

Suddenly another man burst into the room. "I'm General William Davis," the man said. "Who's in charge here?"

Detective Mitchell headed over to speak to him. "I'm Detective Steve Mitchell. I'm heading up this case."

"I've been advised that my kids have been kidnapped in Brazil," the General said. "What are you doing to get them back safely?" Suddenly, Brian had a sickening feeling as to why he was sitting in this room with all of the others.

The detective looked a little intimidated by the General,

but steeled himself. "Please sir, if you could join the others, we'll explain everything." The General paused, then stepped back a few paces to the side. It was obvious he was not going to just sit down with the others. He looked ready to take over the situation if he didn't like what he heard.

Detective Mitchell began his update on the situation. "At approximately 3:00 p.m. yesterday, a tour bus carrying your loved ones and members of your family was intercepted by persons unknown and taken deep into the rainforest in Brazil. About four hours ago, we received notification that they are demanding a ransom of $1 million for the release of each of the victims to be paid by midnight on Saturday, just under seven days from now."

There was a deadly silence, as if all of the oxygen had suddenly been sucked out of the room. Finally, one of the men asked in a quivering voice. "Do we know if they are still alive?"

"We believe so," said Detective Mitchell, "but we've asked for proof of life for each and every person."

"Do you know who the kidnappers are?" someone else asked.

"We believe the kidnappers are members of a group who have staged several similar kidnappings in Brazil over the last few years. The Brazilian police are continuing to investigate. Since this is an international incident involving people from several different countries, there are multiple police agencies involved. The FBI is coordinating activities with the RCMP in North America and we're in continuous communications with other police forces around the world so we have a consistent approach. At this point, we believe we have victims from the United States, Canada, Germany, Japan and Australia."

"Are you recommending that we pay the ransom?" Brian asked.

"At this point, we are not recommending any payment of a ransom because we have no proof of life. If and when we obtain proof of life, it is the policy of the Brazilian government, the United States and the FBI that ransoms not be paid, but the final decision will be left up to each individual."

"If a ransom is paid, who do we pay it to?" someone asked.

"They haven't provided those details yet. Any payment of a ransom should be coordinated through us, or through the respective police force. In similar incidents in the past, the money is transferred to a foreign account which is only active for a short period of time. The funds are normally withdrawn quite quickly after they are transferred which limits our ability to recover or trace the funds."

"What do you think the chances are of them being rescued before the deadline?" Brian asked.

"We can't say for sure," Detective Mitchell said. "We don't have jurisdiction so we are somewhat dependent on the Brazilian police. But we are providing them with whatever assistance we can."

Detective Mitchell paused to see if there were any more questions. "Thank you for your attention," he said to the people in the room. "We'll provide you with any updates as soon as we receive them."

"Well, I'm not going to wait for the fucking Brazilian police," General Davis said as he started to leave the room.

"Please General, we do not have jurisdiction in Brazil," Detective Mitchell said, trying to reason with him.

"I don't care about jurisdiction. I'm going to get my kids back," General Davis said as he stormed by him.

The lady who had been sobbing before was now into a full-scale wail and was rocking back and forth in her chair. Her husband was desperately trying to comfort her.

Brian pulled his cell phone out of his pocket and turned it on. He had turned it off when he had boarded the flight. Once it completed the startup sequence, he hit the keys to call Tom Beamish.

"Brian," Tom said cheerfully when he saw who was calling. "How were the Olympics?"

"Tom," Brian replied. "There's been an incident and I need your help. How quickly can I get my hands on two million dollars?"

Tom immediately sensed the seriousness of the situation, even though he had no idea what was going on. "Consider the money available right now," Tom said. "What's going on?"

"The boys have been kidnapped along with a bunch of other people in Brazil. They're demanding a ransom of one million dollars for the release of each prisoner."

"Where do you want me to send the money?" Tom asked.

"I don't know yet. The FBI is recommending that we not pay the ransom at this point. I just want to make sure the money is available at a moment's notice if we decide to pay the ransom."

"I can have the money sent wherever you want within a matter of seconds. Just say the word and I'll get you whatever you need."

"Thanks Tom," Brian said as he hung up the phone.

Tom sat in stunned silence at his desk. He had known both of those boys since they were born. "Melanie," he yelled to his assistant whose desk was just outside of his office. "I need two million dollars pulled from Brian Baxter's portfolio and placed into our company's trust fund."

"Did you say two million?" Melanie asked. "Will he be coming into the office to sign the paperwork?"

Tom headed out of his office and stood at Melanie's desk. "I'll sign the paperwork," he said. "Just make it happen – now!"

Melanie swallowed hard. She didn't know what was going on but she knew something big was happening. A few minutes later she brought the paperwork into Tom's office. She watched him sign his own name on the line where the investment advisor signs and then felt the colour drain from her face when she saw him sign Brian Baxter's name in the client section. Mr. Beamish was normally such a stickler about getting the proper paperwork and signatures and this was way out of character.

"I want the money there within the hour," Tom said.

*** CHAPTER 15 ***

The sun was barely up but it was already quite steamy underneath the large moldy tarp. Eric had dumped the few remnants out of the plastic first aid kit and was now using it as a cup to bring water to each of the prisoners. "We have to keep drinking water," he said to the Girards as he passed them the water. "If we don't stay hydrated in this heat, we'll die."

"Thanks," Sylvia said. She took a small sip herself and then put the plastic container up to her husband's mouth encouraging him to drain the contents.

Eric took the container back to the water pail, filled it again and took it over to Michael. Michael no longer had a glazed look on his face as he seemed to have recovered somewhat from the ordeal they had been through.

"How's Chip?" he asked Eric.

"A little better, but his leg still looks pretty bad. I think it may be infected because I think he's running a bit of a fever."

Next, Eric took the container filled with water over to an older couple who were huddled together on the ground.

"I'm Eric," he said as he knelt down to give them the water. "It's important that you keep drinking."

"Thanks," the lady said as she helped her husband drink the water. "I'm Anita Taylor and this is my husband Owen."

Owen looked like he was about seventy years old and was looking quite frail and pale. "How are you doing Owen?" Eric asked.

"I'm alright," Owen said as he pulled himself up and shook Eric's hand. Eric felt his hand being squeezed quite firmly but he could tell that Owen was mustering all of his strength to do it. "We're from Texas and I'll be damned if I'm going to let these bastards get the best of me."

"Owen, remember your heart," Anita said. "He's already had a couple of heart attacks and I was worried that trek through the forest was going to cause another one," Anita said to Eric. Although they were old, Eric sensed that this couple were as tough as nails, as long as they had each other for support.

When Eric walked back over to the water pail to fill the plastic container again, two young people walked over to join him. "We need some water as well," the young man said.

"I'm Eric," he said as he handed him the plastic container and watched him down the water in a single gulp. He handed the container to the girl who did the same.

"I'm Jacob Davis," the young man said, "and this is my sister Emily. Is there anything we can do to help?" The two of them barely looked old enough to be out of high school, but they didn't seem frightened at all. "Our father is a General with the U.S. Marines and we're sure our father is planning to rescue us as we speak."

"I hope you're right," Eric said. Eric doubted the U.S. Marines would be organizing a rescue mission in Brazil, but didn't want to dampen their spirits. "We just have to take care of each other until this ordeal is over, so just do what you can." Eric watched as they walked over to sit with the Taylors. Eric sensed the most valuable asset of these two kids would be their positive attitude. He wished he shared their confidence that everything would turn out okay.

Eric continued his deliveries of water to the German couple, the four Japanese tourists and the two Australians. "I hate to be crass," Lucas Williams said, "but where are we supposed to go to the bathroom?"

"I have no idea," Eric replied.

He headed back over to Maria who was now cradling Chip's head and patting his forehead with water trying to cool him off. "Could you ask the guards where we're supposed to go to the bathroom?" Eric asked Maria.

"Okay," Maria said. "I'm also going to ask for some food, some fresh water and a doctor. Your brother has a pretty high fever and he'll die unless he gets some antibiotics."

Maria walked slowly toward one of the gunmen. "Ele precisa de um médico e alguns medicamentos ou outra coisa que ele vai morrer."

The guard walked over to look at Chip with his rifle raised to shoot anyone who approached him. He could easily see that Chip was getting closer and closer to dying.

"Precisamos também de um pouco de comida, água fresca e um lugar para ir ao banheiro.," Maria said to the gunman.

"Você pode ir ao banheiro por baixo do rio, mas apenas dois de cada vez," the gunman replied, holding up two fingers as he said it.

"He said we can go to the bathroom down by the river, but only two people at a time," Maria translated for the group.

Lucas and Oliver Williams were the first to go, with one of the guards watching their every move with his rifle raised, ready to shoot them if they tried to make a run for it. When the two Australians returned, Sylvia Girard helped her husband to his feet and they headed down by the river to do their business. All of the others took their turns in pairs.

"I may have a way for us to escape," Greg whispered to Michael as they walked down the hill toward the river. Greg secretly showed Michael the scissors he had taken from the first aid kit and hidden in his pocket. "I think I can cut through the chicken wire surrounding the complex with these."

"Don't do anything to get us killed," Michael warned.

When they returned to the camp, Greg showed Michael how he had already cut through several links of the chicken-wire fence that surrounded their complex.

However, there was also barbed wire to get through. "There's no way those little scissors are going to be strong enough to cut through the barbed wire," Michael said.

"I don't think we have to," Greg said. He pointed to a break in the barbed wire fence. It looked like it was one long piece of barbed wire, but was actually several pieces that had just been connected together. "All we have to do is untwist these connections," Greg said pointing to the places where they had been joined together.

"Let's ask Eric and Maria what they think," Michael said.

"I'm not sure we can trust Maria," Greg said. "I think Maria and the tour guide might be in on the kidnapping. For all we know, she joined the tour so she could be part of their plan to lure us rich people onto the tour."

Michael had wondered what had happened to the tour guide. She had quickly vanished during the chaos and wasn't one of the hostages. But Michael had no doubts about Maria. "She's not working with the kidnappers. She's the only reason some of us are still alive."

"Well, I know she's poor and I bet she'd do anything not to be poor for the rest of her life."

Michael headed over to discuss the plan with Eric. He mentioned Greg's suspicions about Maria and the tour guide working with the kidnappers.

"Yeah, I was wondering about the tour guide as well," Eric said. "She didn't seem surprised at all about the roadblock." Eric glanced over at Maria who was continuing to tend to Chip. "But there's no way Maria is working with them."

Michael nodded his agreement and they both headed over to discuss the plan with Maria. "Well we can't all make a run for it, but we might be able to sneak one person out of here to go get help without them noticing," Eric said.

"Help is a long way from here," Maria said. "We're in the middle of the rainforest. You'd have to trek several kilometres before you found anyone who could help us."

"I'm sure I could make it," Michael said. "I run over ten kilometres every day, but I don't know which way to go. I'm afraid I'd get lost in this forest."

"Just follow the river," Maria said. "Follow the river until you come to the waterfall. After that, just head through the forest directly toward Pico da Tijuca. That's the highest peak in the forest so you should be able to see it from anywhere. When you get close to it, you should come across some hiking trails which should lead you to a place to get help. There are usually guides leading tourists on hiking tours all around that peak."

"The guards watch us like hawks," Eric said. "We'll need a way to distract them so that Michael can slip away."

"Just leave that to me," Maria said.

*** CHAPTER 16 ***

"We've just heard from the Brazilian police that the kidnappers have announced where they want the money transferred," Detective Mitchell announced to the group. "The account was just created about twenty minutes ago and they indicated that the money must be in that account by 9:00 p.m. tonight for the prisoners to be released."

"I thought we had seven days to pay the ransom," said one of the men from the back of the room. He couldn't hide the panic in his voice.

"That's the final deadline," Detective Mitchell answered. "They say that hostages who have their ransoms paid by 9:00 p.m. tonight will be released within forty eight hours. There will be a different account used tomorrow and a different one every day after that until the final deadline. However, we don't recommend that any ransoms be paid at this time because we still have not received proof of life for any of the prisoners."

Brian didn't know what to do. He approached Detective Mitchell. "What would you do if it was your children who had been kidnapped?"

"I honestly don't know," the detective answered. "If I knew we'd be assured of getting them back, I'd pay the ransom in an instant. But sometimes the kidnappers simply kill the prisoners after they get the money to eliminate any witnesses. I don't mean to be cold, but they may already be dead. That's why I think it's important that we not pay any ransom until we know they're still alive. At that point, we can negotiate the exchange of the money for the prisoners and not just give them the money hoping they will honour the deal."

Brian hung his head and walked out of the meeting room into a long hallway. Detective Mitchell hated having to be so cold in these types of situations, but he knew the statistics and had to follow the most logical plan. He nodded to his partner to go check on Brian.

Brian was staring aimlessly out of the window at the end of the hallway when Detective Johnson came out a few minutes later. "How are you doing?" Detective Johnson asked him. "Is there anything I can get you?"

"Just get my sons back for me," Brian said. He sat down on a padded bench that was in the hallway. "Would you pay the ransom if it was one of your kids?"

The detective sat down on the bench beside him. "I'm not married and I don't have any kids, so I'm probably not a good person to give advice." He paused before continuing. "Unfortunately, there are a lot of kidnappings in Brazil. The Brazilian government discourages the payment of ransoms as a way to discourage these economic kidnappings."

"What do you mean, economic kidnappings?" Brian asked.

"Those are kidnappings that are just done for the money, without any political motivation whatsoever. They've been going on for years in some South American countries like Columbia and Brazil. Columbia used to have the most economic kidnappings of any country in the world so they enacted some laws forbidding the payment of ransoms, hoping that it would stop them. It did help a bit, but now these types of kidnappings are quite common in other countries like Mexico and Brazil. There's no law against paying ransoms in Brazil, but they discourage it." The detective paused before continuing. "Detective Mitchell has to follow FBI policy but to be honest, if it was someone from my family, I'd seriously consider paying the ransom. Don't tell my boss I said that."

"Don't worry," Brian said. "It's nice to know that you think of them as people and not just as another case." Brian gave a heavy sigh. "But I think your boss is right in that as a group we shouldn't give them any money until we get some indication that they're still alive."

"I understand," Detective Johnson said. "You have to do whatever you think is right."

When Detective Johnson went back to the meeting room, he headed over to another couple to try to console them. The FBI had requested that family members of the U.S. kidnap victims all come to Houston to make it easier to manage the situation. "Mr. and Mrs. Porter, how are you holding up?"

"I'm Kevin and this is my wife Lisa", the man said as he shook the detective's hand. "We're not doing so good. We don't have the kind of money to pay the ransom, not even close. I don't know what we're going to do."

"We should have gone with Michael to Brazil," Lisa said. "We went to Beijing to see him compete in 2008 and to London in 2012. It cost us a fortune for those trips and we should have borrowed the money to go watch him compete in Brazil. But Michael said it was okay for us not to go because he didn't think he would win a medal this time."

She shuddered as she took a deep breath. "But then he wins the gold medal and we're not even there to be with him to celebrate. And now we may never see him again." She put her hands over her face and started to rock back and forth.

"Don't give up hope," Detective Johnson said. "The Brazilian police are working to try to find where they are being held and we hope to be able to rescue them without paying any ransom." He put his hand on Lisa's shoulder. "But it's probably a good idea to start figuring out a way to pay the ransom if it comes to that. Who manages your son's sports career?"

Kevin gave the name of his son's agent. "But he's not under contract with anyone right now. Michael had a small contract with Nike after he won the medals in the last two Olympics, but that expired. He was in negotiations for a new contract but they wanted to see how he did in this Olympics before signing him again."

Their conversation was interrupted by Detective Mitchell who was waving at his partner to come speak to him. "Don't worry. I'm confident we'll be able to get your son back to you safe and sound," Detective Johnson said as he headed off.

* * *

"How many people do we still have on the ground in Brazil?" General Davis said into the phone. The General knew that the United States had a lot of marines working undercover in Brazil assisting with security for the Olympics, with the full knowledge and support of the Brazilian government. The General also knew there were even more marines there that the Brazilian government knew nothing about.

"We've already started pulling our people out now that

the Olympics are over," Captain Walmsley replied on the phone, "but we've still got a few there."

"I need a fire team ready for a mission," the General said. "There's been a kidnapping of about twenty people and they're being held somewhere in the rainforests around Rio. Two of the hostages are my kids."

"I understand sir," said the captain. "What do you need?"

"I need satellite surveillance of the area so we can find out where these bastards are hiding," the General said. "And I need the fire team ready to go once we locate them."

"Yes sir," the Captain said.

"And Captain," the General continued, "this is off book."

"Understood sir," the Captain replied.

After he hung up the phone, the General called his ex-wife. He was more afraid of making this call than he had been in all of his years of combat.

"Hilary, it's Bill," he said when she answered.

"I hope you're calling to explain why I haven't received my alimony cheque yet, and don't tell me the cheque's in the mail," Hilary said. "I've heard that excuse too many times to count."

The General took a deep breath before saying what he had to say. "It's about the kids." Hilary immediately sensed that something was wrong. "The kids have been kidnapped in Brazil along with a bunch of other people. They kidnapped all of the people on the tour bus they were on."

Hilary gasped. In a matter of seconds she went from shock to worry to anger. "I told you they were too young to be travelling on their own!!!" she screamed into the phone. "But no, you assured me that everything would be secure and that there'd be nothing to worry about." At that point, she broke down into uncontrollable sobs.

"I'll get them back safe and sound," the General said. "I promise. I've already got a team engaged to rescue them." He wasn't sure she had heard him as all he could hear was her crying.

It was several seconds until Hilary responded. "Your promises don't mean anything to me anymore." Then the phone went dead.

*** CHAPTER 17 ***

Eric and Maria watched as the two Australians lugged the huge wooden bucket of fresh water from the river up to their prison compound. Two of the guards followed about ten paces behind them. They knew how heavy the bucket was – that's why they had the Australians carry it. About twenty minutes later, they arrived again, this time lugging a large basket filled with different kinds of fruit.

"Obrigado, muito obrigado," Maria said as she thanked the guards. Greg looked at Maria suspiciously whenever she spoke to the guards.

Maria started distributing the fruit to everyone. "I don't even know what some of these fruits are called," Eric said.

"This is açaí," Maria said, pointing to something that looked like oversized blueberries, "and this is guarana." She pointed out several more different types of fruit that were native to Brazil and easily found in the rainforest. The basket also contained several pineapples but they couldn't figure out a way to get into them without a knife. Out of frustration, Michael picked up one of the pineapples by the green leaves at the top and whacked it on the top side of the large wooden water pail. After a few more whacks, they could finally get into the juicy fruit inside.

Eric took some of the fruit over to Chip and carefully fed it to him. As he held him, Eric could tell that his fever was higher than before. He knew they were going to have to do something soon or else his brother would die.

The only one who wasn't feasting on the fruit was Greg. He was still suspicious of Maria. The fact that she had convinced the gunmen to bring them food and water only supported his theory that she was in on the kidnapping, at least it did in his mind. Besides, he had work to do. Whenever the guards looked away, he used the scissors to cut another link in the chicken-wire surrounding the compound. However, as the scissors got duller and duller, it was taking longer and longer to cut through each link. But he kept at it at every opportunity until he had created a hole big enough in the chicken wire for a person to crawl through.

After they had eaten, Eric, Maria and Michael had a final chat to confirm the details of their plan. Michael took a few more swigs of water.

"Well, it's show time," Maria whispered to them as she headed over to one of the guards.

"Eu poderia ir até o rio para se banhar?" Maria said. She was confident that they would not object to her heading to the river to bathe.

The eyes of the guard lit up at the prospect. But one of the other guards overheard the request. This was the guard that normally guarded the entrance to the compound and he seemed to be the one in charge as the other guards referred to him as "chefe". "Dois de cada vez," the chief yelled, holding up two fingers.

That was not part of the plan, but Maria figured that it was too late to turn back now. The guard waved his rifle at

Sylvia to join Maria.

"What are we doing?" Sylvia asked Maria as she walked down to the river beside her. They hadn't let everyone in on the plan to try to sneak Michael out of their prison.

"We're going to bathe in the river," Maria whispered. "I'll explain when we get there."

When they got to the river, Maria and Sylvia waded into the river up to their knees. They proceeded to wash their faces and hands. Suddenly, Maria started undoing the buttons down the front of her dress.

"What are you doing?" Sylvia asked. "The guard is right there along the shore. He can see you."

"That's the whole point," Maria whispered to Sylvia. "I'm supposed to distract the guards while Michael tries to escape to go get help." Maria could see out of the corner of her eye that a few more of the guards had moved down along the shoreline.

Up at the camp, Eric watched as more and more of the guards left their posts to head to the river. The only guard left was the chief guarding the main entrance. Michael walked over to sit beside Greg and the two of them pretended to be just talking. Greg positioned himself between Michael and the one remaining guard as Michael secretly started untwisting the links joining the two pieces of barbed wire together. It turned out to be a much tougher task than they thought as the barbed wire was quite thick, but Michael kept at it even though his fingers were now raw and starting to bleed.

Down at the river, Maria took off her dress and handed it to Sylvia to hold. She headed a little farther out into the river, dropped down under the water and when she rose up again, she swirled her long black hair around her as she spun.

"Vem, vem. Ela é quase que completamente nu!" one of

the guards yelled back to the last remaining guard still at his post. This was too much to resist. Seeing a naked woman bathing was worth leaving his post for just a few seconds. The chief took one last look at the prisoners before heading down to the river to join the rest of the guards.

But Maria had to keep them away from their posts for more than a few seconds. She continued to bathe and spent a considerable amount of time washing her breasts, much to the delight of the guards.

Up at the camp, Greg cut the final few links of the chicken-wire fence and pulled the two sections of the barbed wire apart. "Wish me luck," Michael said as he slipped through the opening. Much to his surprise, Greg followed him through the opening. "What are you doing?" Michael asked.

"This was my idea," Greg said. "If anyone deserves to escape, it's me. I'm coming with you."

Michael didn't have time to argue. They both ran off into the forest. Eric moved over and quickly reconnected the barbed wire back together again and pulled the chicken-wire fence together so it was hard to see where the hole was. "Just act normal," Eric said to the other prisoners who had watched what had transpired.

"Should I be doing something?" Sylvia said to Maria down at the river. "I don't think I can take my clothes off knowing that those men are watching."

"You don't have to," Maria said. "Hopefully, we've given Michael enough time to make his escape."

* * *

Michael sprinted through the forest like a gazelle, hardly making a sound as he jumped over logs and small bushes. Greg was lumbering more like a bull and he had already fallen several times. Michael ran back to help Greg to his feet yet again.

"You have to be quiet," Michael whispered. "The camp is only a hundred metres from here and we can't let the guards see or hear us." They had to circle around the camp through the forest and then head back down to the river's edge.

"I'll be faster when we get to the river," Greg whispered.

They reached the river again about five hundred metres upstream from the camp. Michael put out his hand to stop Greg until he was sure it was safe to continue. Greg could see Maria and Sylvia out in the river, but felt sure that the guards wouldn't be able to see them since they were up on the bank and there was a slight bend in the river.

"Okay, I think it's safe to go," Michael said. They started running alongside the river away from the compound at a pretty fast pace.

Maria and Sylvia slowly walked back to the shore where Maria proceeded to put her dress back on. She deliberately spent a long time doing up all of the buttons. They were escorted back to the camp by the guards. Maria was pleased to see that all five guards were part of the escort. She had done her job. She hoped the others had done theirs.

When Maria and Sylvia walked back into the compound, they tried to act as if nothing out of the ordinary had happened. The other prisoners were also trying to make it appear as if nothing had happened while the guards were gone. But Maria couldn't stop herself from doing a quick scan of the surroundings and a small smile crossed her face when she didn't see Michael. She sat with Sylvia for a few minutes before walking over to talk to Eric.

"It looks like Michael got out okay," Maria whispered to Eric. But she could see from the look in Eric's eyes that something had gone wrong.

Eric did a quick look at the guards to make sure they

weren't watching. "Greg went with him," he whispered back to Maria.

Maria's eyes went wide with surprise. When she had looked around the compound for Michael, she hadn't even noticed that Greg had also disappeared. She hoped the guards wouldn't notice either, but she knew the chances of their plan working had instantly dropped by fifty percent, probably more.

The guards hovered around the camp outside the compound discussing their good fortune at being able to watch Maria bathe. Eric couldn't understand what they were saying but he could tell by their gestures that the conversation was pretty crude.

About ten minutes later, Eric knew they were in trouble when he saw the chief start counting the people inside the fence. He whispered to everyone to start moving around figuring it would be harder for him to get an accurate count if they were a moving target. It appeared to work for a while when he saw the chief start his count over again. But when the chief started yelling for the other guards, Eric knew the jig was up.

The chief came into the compound, pointed his rifle directly at Maria and said "Você vai pagar por isso!" He had figured out that Maria's bathing exhibition had been done to distract the guards.

Maria knew full well that she would have to pay for her actions. She just hoped it was all worth it.

* * *

"Wait, I need to take a break," Greg said to Michael after they had run less than a kilometre.

"We don't have time to take a break," Michael said. "We've got to keep going to have any chance of getting away."

Greg was just about to argue with him when they heard the guards yelling. They had obviously just discovered the escape.

Back at the camp, one guard remained behind to watch the prisoners but the other four split up to go searching for Michael and Greg. The guards had no idea which direction they had headed after cutting through the fence. Two guards followed their trail through the forest, which was pretty easy to do given the carnage that Greg had left behind. One guard headed down the river and the fourth guard headed upstream. It was only a few minutes later when one of the guards found Greg and Michael's tracks alongside the river and he called to the other guards.

Michael figured he was about two kilometres ahead of the guards and he was sure he could run faster than they could. But Greg couldn't. He was already into a slow jog and stopped several times to catch his breath. "I just need a minute to rest," Greg said as he sat down once again on the river bank. "And I need a drink. It's so hot." Greg cupped his hands to get a drink from the river and then splashed some water over his face.

"We have to keep going," Michael said in frustration. "I'm sure the guards will have picked up our trail by now."

Greg looked back down the river. "I don't see anyone. Maybe they're looking for us in the rainforest."

Michael didn't think they would be that lucky. He pulled Greg up to his feet. "We have to keep going. They're all counting on us to find help."

They started running along the river again and after about five minutes, Michael thought he could hear the sound of the waterfall up ahead. He looked back and saw Greg several hundred metres behind him. Michael debated leaving him behind, but when he saw Greg stumble over some rocks and crash head first into the river, he decided to head back to help him. Michael had just reached Greg when he heard the sound of a rifle being cocked.

"Não se mova," said the chief.

Michael froze in his spot and put his hands up to surrender. But Greg got up and started running into the river.

"Parar ou vou chutar!" the chief yelled.

But Greg kept running out into the river. The chief fired a shot over Greg's shoulder which hit the water just a few feet in front of him, but Greg still didn't stop. The next shot hit him square in the back of the head. The water turned a crimson red as Greg's limp body moved back downstream toward them. A couple more guards came running up.

"Obtenha o corpo," the chief yelled to his partners. They waded into the river and dragged Greg's body back to shore.

Michael was pretty sure that Greg was already dead but when the guards flipped his body over, the chief fired another shot into him just to be sure. Michael sank to his knees and started throwing up. He was pretty sure his fate was sealed as well.

Back at the compound, the rest of the prisoners cringed when they heard the two gunshots. Eric and Maria looked at each other and knew that their plan had failed. Maria fell to her knees and said a short prayer.

As darkness started to fall over the compound, an eerie silence also spread everywhere. There was no rustling of trees in the breeze. No sounds of birds or animals in the forest. This was the sound of death.

*** CHAPTER 18 ***

Eric was awakened the next morning by the scuffling he heard going on outside of their compound. He could hear someone being beaten and he didn't know whether to be happy or sad when one of the guards brought Michael back into the compound and threw him to the ground.

Eric and Maria immediately headed over to take care of Michael. He had been beaten quite badly, but he was thankfully still alive. "I'm sorry, we failed," Michael gasped before he lost consciousness.

Maria headed over to the water pail, tore another strip off of her dress and headed back to Michael to tend to his wounds. Eric could hear another man being beaten and he wondered whether it was Greg.

"Você não deveria ter deixado o seu post!" shouted one of the men. When he looked out through the wire fence that surrounded their prison compound, Eric was surprised to see that the chief was the one being beaten by a new man that had arrived in camp. Eric could see at least two new guards that hadn't been there the day before. They had obviously brought in reinforcements after the attempted escape the day before.

One of the new men came walking into the compound. Like the others, he was wearing a mask to cover his face, but his was a surgical mask rather than the bandanas worn by the other guards.

"Onde está o homem que precisa de médico?" he asked Maria.

"Aqui," Maria said as she led him over to where Chip was lying.

Eric headed over to watch. Although he knew Chip desperately needed a doctor, he wasn't going to just let a butcher with a surgical mask treat him.

The doctor carefully removed the bandages that Maria had applied a couple of days earlier. "Você é o único que tratou as feridas?" the doctor asked Maria.

"Sim, eu fiz o melhor que pude," Maria said.

"What is he saying?" Eric asked Maria, trying to figure out what was going on.

"I asked if she was the one who treated his wounds," the doctor said in flawless English. "She did a great job with what she had." He opened his bag which was filled with medical supplies. "I'm going to give him some penicillin because he's got an infection and I'm going to have to stitch up his leg."

Eric watched as he first gave Chip the penicillin injection and then a few more small needles to freeze his leg. As he watched him work, Eric could tell he was a skilled doctor. Chip's leg required a lot of stitches and the doctor did it with a precision only someone who had been well trained could do. Eric glanced inside the doctor's bag and noticed several items that had the UCLA logo.

"Are you American?" Eric asked.

The doctor laughed. "No," he replied, "but I went to medical school at UCLA. I wanted to practice medicine in the U.S. after I finished school, but they kicked me out of the country." He glanced up to look Eric in the eye. "But don't worry, I know what I'm doing."

Eric could easily see that he did. "We've got another guy over here with a banged up shoulder you should probably take a look at," Eric said after the doctor finished stitching up Chip's leg. Eric led him over to where Jean-Pierre Girard was lying, still cradling his shoulder.

"Let me take a look at that shoulder," the doctor said to Jean-Pierre. Sylvia was still holding on to her husband and seemed reluctant to let go.

"It's okay," Eric said to her. "He seems to know what he's doing."

"This is for the pain," the doctor said as he gave Jean-Pierre an injection. "This should help, but I'll be back in a few minutes to check on you again."

"What about Michael?" Maria asked the doctor as she tended to him.

"He'll be alright," the doctor said. "He shouldn't have tried to escape. He's lucky the guards didn't beat him any worse."

Eric wanted to ask about Greg, but then thought maybe he and Michael had split up and that Greg had made it out undiscovered. Eric didn't want to let the guards know that two people had snuck out of camp if they didn't already know.

Eric led the doctor around to see the other prisoners. However, they only had minor cuts and scrapes so were easily treated.

"That fellow over there has a dislocated shoulder," the doctor whispered to Eric as he glanced back over to Jean-Pierre. "The pain killer will help but we should really try to put his shoulder back in place. It's going to hurt like hell and I'll need a couple of people to help."

Eric waved to Maria who came over to join them. "Just tell us what to do," Eric said.

"How's your shoulder feeling now?" the doctor asked Jean-Pierre when the three of them headed back over to where he was lying on the ground.

"A lot better," Jean-Pierre replied. "The pain killer you gave me sure seemed to help."

"Yeah, that should ease the pain," the doctor said, "but you have a dislocated shoulder and we should really try to put it back into place."

He asked Jean-Pierre to sit up and he instructed Eric and Maria where to hold Jean-Pierre. "Okay, on three," he said to them as he gently started moving Jean-Pierre' shoulder in a circular motion.

"One," he said. Suddenly he pushed on Jean-Pierre's shoulder as he pulled on his arm. Jean-Pierre let out a piercing scream and he blacked out for a few seconds.

"Two, three," the doctor said quickly. "It's best if he not know when it's going to happen," he said in explanation. He gave Jean-Pierre another injection for the pain. "I think he should be alright now."

The doctor walked with Eric and Maria back over to where Chip was lying. "I'll be back tomorrow to check on him," the doctor said. "Do you want me to take a look at that ankle?" he asked Eric as they were walking. He had noticed that Eric seemed to be in pain as he walked.

"No," Eric said. "It's just gout. I'll be fine. I shouldn't have eaten all of that seafood at the tour dinner."

Suddenly, one of the new guards came into the complex. "Onde estão os alemães?" he yelled to no one in particular.

Maria ran over and stood in front of the German couple who were cowering in fear. Eric ran over and stood beside her. The guard raised his rifle and pointed it at Eric and Maria. "Quando você está tomando?" Maria asked.

"Their ransom has been paid," the doctor said trying to keep everyone calm. "They are being released."

* * *

"Could I have everyone's attention?" Detective Mitchell said to the people who were scattered around the room. Brian was out in the hallway sitting on the leather bench, but headed back into the meeting room when he heard Detective Mitchell.

"We've just been informed that the German police have authorized the payment of the ransom for three of the hostages. Last night, ransoms were paid for Klaus and Anja Weber and Greg Schneider."

"Should we be paying the ransoms for the others?" Brian asked.

"We don't recommend paying any ransoms at this point," Detective Mitchell said. "We still don't know if any of the hostages are alive. The kidnappers have said they will release a hostage within forty eight hours of their ransom being paid. I recommend that we wait to see if they honour the deal for the first three hostages before we decide on our next course of action."

"We couldn't pay the ransom, even if we wanted to," said the man sitting next to Brian.

Brian didn't know if the man was talking to him or just voicing his frustrations out loud. "It's hard to know what to do," Brian said in response.

"I'm Jamie Taylor," the man said reaching out his hand to Brian, "and this is my sister Sarah." They both looked in their mid-thirties and it was easy to see the family resemblance. "It's our parents who have been kidnapped. This was supposed to be their trip of a lifetime and the start of their trip around the world."

Jamie and Sarah were struggling to come up with a way

to save their parents. "This ordeal will be too much for dad," Sarah said. "His heart won't be able to take it."

"Don't say that!" Jamie scolded his sister. "He's pretty tough!" He stood up and started to pace back and forth.

Detective Johnson heard the raised voices and came over to offer his help. "How's everyone doing over here?" he asked as he approached.

"We don't have the money to pay the ransom," Jamie said, "and we don't know what to do."

"Well, remember that we're not recommending the payment of any ransom at this point, but it's probably a good idea to start planning for that contingency," the detective said. Detective Johnson pulled up a chair so that he could talk with the Taylor kids a little more privately, but Brian couldn't help but overhear their conversation.

"Do you have any stocks or property that you could sell?" the detective asked them.

"How much money do you think we could get if we both remortgaged our houses?" Jamie asked his sister.

"I have no idea," Sarah said.

"I'd suggest you find out," the detective said, "but don't sign anything yet. At this point, we're recommending that everyone wait until we know they're still alive."

Brian gave a heavy sigh. The last thing he wanted to do was wait. He headed back out into the hallway and laid down on the leather bench underneath the window. Although the FBI had arranged for rooms for everyone at a nearby hotel, Brian had effectively camped out on the leather bench in the hallway at FBI headquarters. He was afraid to go to the hotel in case he missed any updates about his sons. He stared out the window and watched the clouds as they drifted slowly across the sky. The clouds were gradually getting darker and darker as it looked like a major storm was approaching. Brian was exhausted as he hadn't slept very much at all over the last few days. As he watched the clouds drift by, he gradually fell asleep.

"Don't you let them take my babies away from me," his wife said to him in his dream.

"I don't know what to do," Brian said. "The FBI detective said we shouldn't pay any ransoms until we find out if the first three hostages have been released alive."

"They're not his kids," Jean said. "They're ours, and you promised me you'd take care of them for me."

"I know. I just wish I knew if they were still alive."

"They are. I can feel it in my soul, but you're going to have to do something soon to save them. They're running out of time."

Brian was jolted awake by a huge crack of thunder and a bolt of lightning that hit almost simultaneously. Houston was now in the midst of a major thunderstorm and the lightning strike had just knocked out the power in the building.

"Don't worry," Brian heard Detective Mitchell shout from inside the meeting room. "We have a backup generator and the power should be back on within a minute or two."

Sure enough, the lights came back on in the meeting room within a few seconds. Brian headed out of the darkened hallway and back into the meeting room. He saw a woman crying by herself at the back of the room. He remembered her from the first time he had arrived at FBI headquarters. "I'm sure everything will turn out okay," Brian said trying to console her.

"No it won't," she said. "My husband is refusing to pay any ransom."

"The FBI doesn't want us to pay any additional ransoms until we know if the three German hostages have been released unharmed," Brian said. "I'm sure your husband will pay to have your son or daughter released once we know."

"It's my daughter Sylvia and her husband Jean-Pierre that have been kidnapped," the woman said. "I'm Elizabeth Noble," she said as she wiped the tears from her face, "and that's my husband who is putting on his coat to leave." Brian looked toward the front of the room and could see the man talking to Detective Mitchell. He finished putting on his coat and then left.

"I'm Brian Baxter," Brian said to the woman. "It's a stressful time for all of us," he continued, trying to reassure her. "I'm sure he'll be back. Tell me about your daughter."

"Sylvia is our only child," Elizabeth said. "She's been my whole life. She was backpacking across Europe with some of her classmates after they finished college when she met Jean-Pierre in France. At first, we thought it was just a summer romance but he followed her back to the States. My husband never really approved and I didn't really at first either, but I could see that Sylvia was madly in love with him. My husband was convinced that he was just after our money. When they told us they were getting married, my husband told Sylvia that he'd cut her off if she went through with it. I think he thought they'd call the wedding off. But they didn't and now they've got two kids that I've never even seen."

Elizabeth broke into an uncontrollable sob. Brian put his arm around her to console her but she continued to cry and cry. "I'm so sorry," she said after about five minutes. She pulled herself away from Brian and tried to compose herself. "Here I am going on about my problems and you've got one of your own family that's been kidnapped."

"Two actually," Brian said. "My two sons Eric and Chip were kidnapped."

"I'm so sorry," Elizabeth said. "Tell me about them."

"Well Eric is my oldest," Brian said. "He just finished school up in Canada, which is where we're from, and just started his career as a financial planner. Chip is my youngest son and he's an Olympic athlete, which is why we were in Brazil."

"I can tell you're proud of both of them," Elizabeth said.

"They mean the world to me," Brian said.

Brian looked at the front of the room and saw Elizabeth's husband coming back in. "See, I told you he'd be back. He probably just went for a walk to relieve some of the stress."

"I hope you're right," Elizabeth said. "Thanks for listening to me," she said reaching out to touch Brian's hand.

"We all have to stick together to get through this," Brian said.

*** CHAPTER 19 ***

Eric and Maria watched as the guard placed hoods over the heads of the German couple. They were tied together with about ten feet of rope and headed off into the forest with one guard at the front and the doctor trailing behind.

They walked for several kilometres through the forest. However, they didn't fall as much as they had on their journey there as the doctor warned them about logs or bushes that could cause them to trip. After their trek, they were loaded into a small jeep which drove for several more kilometres through the rainforest. The jeep stopped just before they came to a trail, if you could call it that, but it at least had tire tracks from other vehicles that had gone the same way.

"We're going to remove your hoods," the doctor said, "but don't attempt to call out if you see anyone or the guard will shoot you. We've still got a long way to go." The guard had the rifle sitting on his lap pointed at the two hostages.

They continued driving down the trail which eventually connected to a main road. The German couple were filled with hope as the jeep drove down the main road as they could tell they were getting closer and closer to civilization again. But their hope instantly turned to fear again as the jeep turned off the main road and onto another trail that headed back into another part of the rainforest. Suddenly the jeep slowed down in the middle of nowhere and then turned around in a small clearing.

The guard pointed the rifle at them and waved for them to get out of the jeep. "Please don't kill us," Klaus said as he held his wife tightly in his arms, putting his body between her and the gunman. "We didn't see your faces and we won't say a word, I promise." He could see that the gunman didn't understand a word he was saying and his eyes showed that he didn't care. Klaus was sure they were going to be executed and left for dead in the forest.

"Just follow this trail back to the main road," the doctor said. "It's about ten kilometres so it will take you a while to get there. You should be able to flag down someone on that road who will take you to safety. Good luck."

The jeep then sped off down the trail. Klaus and Anja Weber just stood there hugging each other for several minutes. They were together, alive and free. They each took a deep breath as they started their walk back toward civilization and the rest of their lives.

* * *

About two hours after the German couple had been led off into the forest, Eric and Maria heard some shouting among the guards. Suddenly the chief guard came walking into the compound with his rifle raised. His face was badly bruised and scarred. He was obviously the one that had been beaten for leaving his post. As he approached, he raised his rifle and pointed it directly at Maria.

"É hora de você pagar, você cadela!" he yelled at Maria.

Eric jumped to his feet and stood between Maria and the chief. But another guard came into the compound and positioned his rifle just a few inches from Eric's head.

"Ela vai ser o que ela merece!" the guard yelled at Eric. Eric had no idea what was going on.

"It's alright," Maria said to Eric. "They can't hurt me." She lied, because she knew exactly what the guards were going to do but she didn't want Eric to get shot on her behalf.

The guards led Maria down toward the river. They stopped by a tree and tied her hands above her head to an overhanging branch. The chief put down his rifle and started to undo his pants. Maria tried to kick him in the groin but he caught her leg before it reached its target. As he held her leg, he slid his hand up under her dress until he found the prize he was looking for. The other guard put down his rifle and grabbed Maria's other leg so she couldn't try to kick them again. The chief pulled a knife from his boot and held it up to Maria's throat. He nicked her throat with the knife, just enough to draw a trickle of blood. But then he moved the knife down and cut the buttons off of Maria's dress one by one, throwing her dress wide open when the last button went flying to the ground.

Maria closed her eyes as the chief dropped his pants to his ankles. But he grabbed her by the throat and forced her to look at him. "Quero olhar nos seus olhos enquanto eu estupro você, cadela!"

Maria tried to go numb. She could see the evil in this man's eyes but she was determined not to let him see the fear she was feeling inside. He gave a sinister smile as he was about to drive himself into her. But then his expression changed. The smile turned into a look of confusion. His eyes showed a brief moment of pain, but then just became cold and blank. He slid to the ground in front of her.

Maria had become numb. She hadn't heard the gunshot that had just taken the life of the chief. But she heard the gunshot that took out the second guard. Suddenly, another man was standing in front of her. This man wasn't wearing a mask like the guards. She didn't recognize him but she could see the kindness in his eyes. "Você está bem?" he asked.

She recognized the voice. The doctor had returned just in time to save her.

*** CHAPTER 20 ***

"We'd like everyone back in the meeting room," Detective Johnson said to Brian. "We've got some updates to give everyone." Brian headed back into the meeting room and could see several of the TV screens in the room lit up showing people from other countries. The first screen was showing a feed from the Japanese police headquarters, the second from German police force, the third from Australia and the last from Brazil.

The detective was just about to begin his update when a lady that Brian had never seen before came walking into the room. "Welcome, Mrs. Davis," Detective Mitchell said to the woman. "Yes, we've got an update. Please take a seat with the others." She took the seat beside Brian and he could see her clutching a picture of herself, General Davis and their two kids.

The Australian police were the first to give an update. "We'd like to report that the two million dollar ransom has been paid for Oliver and Lucas Williams from Sydney Australia," the detective from Australia said. "The money was transferred to the account specified approximately two hours ago. We've been monitoring it and the money was removed from that account twenty two minutes ago. We are in the process of tracing where the money went after it left the account."

The Japanese police were the next to report. "Against our recommendations," the Japanese officer said, "the Takahashi corporation paid a ransom of four million dollars for the release of four of their executives. They indicated they carry insurance to cover such events for their key executives."

"I thought we had agreed that we would not pay any additional ransoms until we found out if the first three hostages were released unharmed," Detective Mitchell said. He was clearly frustrated that those agreements had been ignored.

"The ransoms for the Takahashi executives were paid against our recommendations," the Japanese officer reiterated.

"We expressed our concerns," the Australian detective said, "but in the end, we felt it was up to the family to decide whether to pay the ransom or not."

Brian's heart sank in his chest. He wished he had just paid the ransom for his sons. It would destroy him if his inaction had cost his sons their lives.

"Are there any updates on the status of the German hostages?" Detective Mitchell asked the Brazilian police. "It has now been almost forty eight hours since their ransoms were paid."

"We've just received word that two German people were found wandering through the forest by a local hiker," the Brazilian police officer reported. "At this point, we don't know if they are two of the hostages or just two tourists who got separated from their tour."

"Only two?" the German officer asked. "Ransoms were

paid for three hostages from Germany."

"Yes, only two people were found," confirmed the Brazilian police officer. "That's why we're not sure if they are two of the hostages or not. They do not appear to have been injured but they have been taken to a local hospital to be examined. We expect to have further information available within the hour. I recommend we reconvene at that time."

"Agreed," Detective Mitchell said, "One hour from now. Once we know if they are the hostages, we'll determine our plans going forward." The TV screens showing the participants from the other parts of the world went black.

"I want to pay the ransom for my sons right now," Brian said to Detective Mitchell.

"I understand how you feel," Detective Mitchell said. "But we've still got three days until the final deadline. Just give me two more hours to find out the status of the German hostages. If they've been released unharmed, I'll support your decision to pay the ransom."

"Listen to me," Brian yelled at him, grabbing the detective by his shirt collar. "I want to pay the fucking ransom right now! I've waited long enough. I've got to get my boys back!"

"You can't right now," Detective Mitchell said trying to reason with him. "They haven't given us the account yet to be used for the next payment. The account used for yesterday's payments has already been closed."

Brian looked like he was about to punch him, but Detective Johnson intervened to try to calm the situation. "Mr. Baxter, I think it's best if you take a walk to try to calm down." Brian released his grip on Detective Mitchell and headed to the hallway outside of the meeting room.

"I have some additional information," Detective Johnson whispered to his partner after Brian had left. "I just received word that one of the sports management companies paid the ransom for Michael Porter last night."

"You've got to be fucking kidding me!" Detective Mitchell said loudly. The other people in the room looked at him wondering what had gone wrong. He quickly lowered his voice again to a whisper. "They didn't pay the ransom into the account we were given or else I would have known about it."

"I know," Detective Johnson whispered back. "They somehow had another account to be used and they transferred the ransom to that account last night. They said they have negotiated a huge endorsement deal for Mr. Porter because he won the Olympic gold medal and the deal is worth millions to them."

Detective Mitchell became even more frustrated. He knew he was going to have trouble controlling people from other countries, but he now realized he had even lost control of those on his own soil.

*** CHAPTER 21 ***

"Você está bem?" the doctor asked Maria again as he cut the ropes that tied her to the overhanging branch. Maria didn't reply but just held him.

The other guards had come running when they had heard the gunshots. "Voltar para suas postagens!" the doctor yelled at them when they got there. They could see the dead bodies of two of the other guards, but lowered their rifles and headed back to their posts.

The doctor held Maria for several minutes as she trembled. She refused to cry but she could not stop the trembling no matter how hard she tried. The doctor pulled her dress closed around her and then used a piece of the rope to tie it together around her waist. He pulled his surgical mask up over his face and then helped her make her way back to the compound.

The other hostages had heard the gunshots and feared the worst. They were all relieved when they saw Maria was still alive. "I think she's okay," the doctor said as he passed Maria over to Eric who tried to comfort her. "I think I got there before they hurt her."

"Oh my God Maria, are you alright?" Sylvia Girard said as she came running over to help take care of her. Maria was still trembling as Sylvia held her and took her over to the other side of the compound.

The doctor looked directly into Eric's eyes. "I'm sorry," he said. "If it makes you feel any better, I killed both of the guards involved."

It should have made him feel better, but for some reason, it didn't. Eric felt his spirit dropping and could sense that the morale within the other hostages was dropping as well. Chip's condition was better since the doctor had treated him, but he was still very weak. Michael had regained consciousness but the guards had beaten him so badly that he was barely able to talk or move. Mr. Taylor was looking like he could have another heart attack at any moment. And Eric couldn't even bear to think about what had happened to Maria.

Eric took a deep breath and headed over to talk to Jacob and Emily Davis. "How confident are you that your father will be sending a team of marines to rescue us?" he asked Jacob.

"I can guarantee it, sir," Jacob answered as if he was a marine himself.

"Well, I'd like you two to let the others know that help is on the way," Eric said. "We've got to give everyone hope that everything is going to turn out okay."

"Consider it done," Jacob said without any hesitation.

"But do it quietly," Eric said. "I don't want to alert the guards that a rescue team is on the way."

Eric watched as Jacob and Emily Davis went from person to person telling them about their father's rescue operation. He could see each person's spirit lift as they were told. However, when they tried to approach Maria and Sylvia, Sylvia waved them away. Sylvia continued to hold Maria as she cried.

Eric desperately wanted to help Maria but he wasn't sure what he should do. He wandered over and sat down on the ground near them. Although he didn't say or do anything, he just wanted to be close to Maria to let her know that he was there for her.

* * *

The next morning one of the guards came into the compound and waved his rifle at the four Japanese men. "O resgate foi pago," the guard said. The four men looked confused.

"Your ransom has been paid," the doctor said to the four Japanese men. "You are being released. The ransom has also been paid for the two Australians," the doctor said pointing to them, "and also for the U.S. Olympic athlete."

Michael struggled to get to his feet as the bruises that he had received in the beating were now apparent. He wondered whether one of his ribs might also be broken. He headed over to help Chip to his feet. Chip was looking a lot better today as the infection in his leg seemed to be getting better and he no longer had a fever. "We're both Olympic athletes for the U.S. team," Michael said.

"Sorry," the doctor said, "but the million dollar ransom was only paid for one of you. The one who won the gold medal."

"I'm not leaving here without Chip," Michael said, looking defiant. "We're team-mates."

"Are you sure you really want to do that?" the doctor asked. "It could cost you your life."

"Don't be stupid," Chip said to Michael. "They've paid your ransom so don't pass up this opportunity to get out of here. Besides, I'm not going anywhere without my brother."

Michael looked torn. "Why would they pay the ransom for me and not you?" he asked in frustration.

"Because you're the U.S. Olympic gold medalist," Chip said.

"Not anymore," Michael said. He pulled the gold medal from underneath his shirt and put it around Chip's neck. "I'll be back to get you out of here, one way or another. I promise."

The rest of the hostages watched as the guards led Michael, the four Japanese men and the two Australians out into the forest and to their freedom.

*** CHAPTER 22 ***

Detective Mitchell looked at his watch while waiting in the meeting room. The TV screens showing the policemen from Germany, Australia and Japan were lit up for the video conference. They were still waiting for the Brazilians to join and it was now five minutes past the scheduled time for the conference.

"I understand that we've found some of the hostages," General Davis said when he stormed into the meeting room.

"Please sit down with the others," Detective Mitchell said, trying to remain in control of the room. "We're waiting for the Brazilian police to confirm whether the people they found are, in fact, two of the hostages." The general and the detective glared at each other. Although the detective was supposed to be in charge of this case, the General had never been comfortable with being second in command of anything.

The General noticed that his ex-wife was one of the people sitting in the room waiting for an update. This seemed to surprise him as he thought he had made it quite clear to her that he would be taking care of the situation. Mrs. Davis shook her head in derision. She had seen her husband exhibit this controlling behavior too many times to count. Fortunately, the confrontation between Detective Mitchell and the General was interrupted by the TV screen showing the feed from Brazil coming to life.

The monitor showed the officer from Brazil along with the two people who had been found. "I'd like to introduce Klaus and Anja Weber, two of the German hostages who have been released." They looked worn and tired, but in pretty good health, all things considered.

"We're glad to see that you're safe," the policeman from Germany said. "Do we know the status of Gregory Schneider?"

"We believe he was killed," the Brazilian officer said. "I'll let Mr. Weber provide the details."

"We think Greg was killed trying to escape," Mr. Weber said. "Greg and Michael cut their way through the wire fence and tried to escape into the forest the day before we were released. We heard a couple of gunshots after they escaped and they only brought Michael back to the camp."

As they listened, Kevin and Lisa Porter hugged each other knowing that their son was still alive.

"We think Greg was shot by the guards but we never saw his body," continued Mr. Weber. "We hope we're wrong and that he got away."

"We hope so too," Detective Mitchell said. "If possible, we'd like you to confirm the identities of the people who were kidnapped along with you." The police had obtained a list of names from the manager at the hotel of the people who were supposed to be on the tour.

"We'll try," Mr. Weber said, "but we don't really know the others. We just met them on the tour."

"I understand," Detective Mitchell said, "but we've got

some pictures of the people who we believe were kidnapped." The first two pictures they were shown were Lucas and Oliver Williams.

Mr. Weber squinted to see the pictures that were displayed on the screen. "I think those are the two Australians," Mr. Weber said. He looked at his wife for confirmation. "Yes, they were kidnapped as well."

The next pictures displayed were the four Japanese executives. The pictures they had of them showed them dressed in business suits. "I know there were four Japanese men that were kidnapped, but I don't know if that's them or not. They look so different in those pictures."

They showed them pictures of Jean-Pierre and Sylvia Girard, Owen and Anita Taylor, and Jacob and Emily Davis. "I remember Jean-Pierre Girard for sure," Mr. Weber said, "because he hurt his shoulder. I think the others were there as well."

"Were Jacob and Emily Davis hurt in any way?" General Davis interrupted.

"I don't think so," Mr. Weber said. Hilary Davis let out a thankful sigh when she heard the news.

The next pictures displayed were for Eric and Chip. "Oh, that's Eric," Mr. Weber said immediately. "I know that he's one of the hostages. He was one of the people who was trying to take care of us all. He brought all of us water. I think the other one is the kid who was really badly injured."

Brian could hardly breathe when he heard that. Detective Johnson put his hand on Brian's shoulder to try to console him. "What type of injury did he have?" the detective asked.

"He had a huge gash on his leg from the barbed wire," Mr. Weber said. "I know that Eric was really worried that he was going to die because it got infected. But Eric and

Maria convinced the guards to get him a doctor so I know he got treated before we were released."

"Who's Maria?" Detective Mitchell asked. "We don't have anyone named Maria listed as one of the hostages."

"I think she worked at the hotel," Mr. Weber said. "She was on the tour bus with Greg."

"We might all be dead if it wasn't for Maria," Anja Weber said. "She was the only one who understood what the guards were saying. It was Maria and Eric who convinced the guards to get a doctor and to bring us food and water."

Detective Mitchell started taking notes to try to get additional information as to who Maria was. "Can you tell us anything about the doctor?" Detective Mitchell asked.

"Only that he was a very good doctor," Mr. Weber said. "Eric said he did a great job stitching up his brother's leg and he fixed Jean-Pierre Girard's shoulder with help from Eric and Maria. I think he might have been American."

Detective Mitchell seemed surprised by that last statement and was going to pursue it further, but General Davis interrupted and asked the next question. "Can you describe the location where you were being held?"

"We were close to a river, but a long way into the rainforest," Mr. Weber said. "They put hoods over our heads so we couldn't see anything, but we walked for several kilometres through the forest before they loaded us into a jeep, and then we drove down a path for several more kilometres before we came to anything you could really call a road. We thought they were going to take us into the city but they took us back out into the forest. We thought we were going to kill us." He reached over and gave his wife a reassuring hug.

The Brazilian police officer displayed a map showing the area with a red "X" marking where the Webers had been found. General Davis focused in on the map. "Could you send us a copy of that map?" the General asked. Detective Mitchell glared at the General for taking over the meeting, but knew that the map might be useful in determining where the hostages were being held.

"What did the camp look like?" Detective Mitchell asked.

"Well, like I already said, it is close to a small river because they would let us go there to go to the bathroom. The camp was like a huge tent with brownish-green tarps over the top. The walls were made of a wire fence with barbed wire running through it."

After they had answered all of the questions, the Brazilian police officer thanked the Webers for all of the information they had provided. "We're hoping that the information you have provided will help us locate the rest of the hostages."

General Davis had already left the room. With a map and the information that he now had, he was confident that his marines would be able to rescue his son and daughter.

*** CHAPTER 23 ***

Michael hated having the hood over his head as he marched through the forest along with the two Australians and the four Japanese men. It made him feel so claustrophobic and he desperately wanted to rip it off of his head to relieve the fear that was growing inside of him. But he knew that the guards would probably shoot him if he did. He tried to focus his thoughts on just taking one stride after another, something he had done countless times during races when he was fighting the pain he felt in his legs and his lungs. But this was different. The problem was inside his head. He pretended he was running the 10,000 metre event and counting down the strides required to complete the race. He desperately hoped they would reach the end of their march through the forest before he reached zero.

The two Australians who were tied to the rope in front of Michael were also fighting their own fears. But they would periodically whisper encouragement to each other. "It won't be long until we're back on the beach in Australia," Lucas whispered to his brother.

"On our surf boards," Oliver whispered back. Oliver

imagined the cool spray of the surf to try to block out the stifling heat they felt in the rainforest.

The four Japanese men that were tied to the rope behind Michael followed along like soldiers. They didn't seem to need to communicate with each other to offer encouragement. It was almost like it was their duty to persevere through this hardship without complaint.

"Pare de andar!" yelled one of the guards and they all came to a stop.

Michael felt himself being pulled forward as the two Australians in front of him climbed into the back of a military-style truck. He crawled on his hands and knees along the bed of the truck and collapsed beside the Australians. However, as the four Japanese men crawled into the truck, Michael found himself being pulled backwards by the rope that tied them all together. As he did, he felt the hood start to slip off the top of his head, not all the way, but enough so that he could see out of the bottom of the hood by looking down. He really couldn't see anything but the truck bed but it helped to relieve his feelings of claustrophobia.

Suddenly the truck started up and they drove for what seemed like an incredibly long time. They were being tossed around on the bed of the truck with every bump they hit in the road. And with every bump, Michael was reminded once again of the beating he had received from the guards. The cracked rib and bruises throbbed with every jarring bump. However, he knew he was lucky to be alive. They could have just shot him and left his body alongside the river like they had with Greg.

As Michael laid there getting jostled around, he realized that he could see the guard that was sitting in the back of the truck through the opening in the bottom of his hood. The guard briefly removed the bandana covering his face to wipe the sweat from his face and neck. Michael knew it was a face he would never forget.

* * *

Back at the compound, Sylvia continued to try to comfort Maria. "I'm okay," Maria said. "The doctor shot them before they could hurt me." She was starting to regain her composure.

Gradually, the hostages started to congregate in the centre of the compound. After Michael, the two Australians and the four Japanese men had been released, the others seemed to move closer together to support each other. "Did the doctor say they paid a million dollar ransom to have Michael released?" Owen Taylor asked.

"Yeah, I think so," Eric replied. "I suspect that there's a million dollar ransom for each of us. They probably targeted the tour bus because they knew people on the tour were pretty wealthy."

"Well, we're pretty well off," Owen said, "but our family doesn't have two million dollars to pay in ransom for me and my wife." Owen hugged his wife before continuing on. "We're over sixty five years old now and this was supposed to be our vacation of a lifetime. We've been saving for this trip for several years and it was supposed to be the start of our trip around the world. Instead...," he started to say, but then didn't finish his thought. "How about you? Do you have someone who'll be willing to pay a million dollars for your release?

"Yeah," Eric said. "My dad. Actually, it would be two million dollars for Chip and myself."

"How about you?" Owen asked, looking at Jean-Pierre and Sylvia Girard. "Does your family have money?"

Jean-Pierre and Sylvia looked at each other before deciding whether to answer. "Sylvia's family is quite wealthy," Jean-Pierre said, "but they cut her off from their money when she married me six years ago. They didn't approve of our marriage so they were hoping to use that as leverage to break us up. It didn't work and we haven't taken a cent of their money since. We do okay on our own. I make enough to take care of Sylvia and our two kids."

"Yes, but surely they would pay the ransom to get you back with their grandchildren, whether they approved of your marriage or not," Owen said.

Sylvia started to cry. "We don't let them see their grandchildren," she confessed. Maria came over to comfort Sylvia. Maria had dreamed of having the life that Jean-Pierre and Sylvia had, but was now realizing it was not perfect either.

"I'm pretty sure we'll be rescued before any more ransoms are paid," Jacob Davis said. Eric was pleased to hear Jacob voice a more positive outlook. Jacob had been pretty reserved during their entire ordeal, but he always seemed on alert waiting for something to happen. His sister, Emily, had also exhibited a quiet confidence that everything was going to turn out alright, but her resolve seemed a bit more fragile than her brother's. Everyone hoped that they were right.

*** CHAPTER 24 ***

"General Davis," Captain Walmsley said into the phone. "We believe we've identified the location where the hostages are being held. Requesting permission to engage, sir."

"Approved," General Davis said, "but I'll be supervising the operation personally." It was less than a minute later when the General walked through the door of the control room. "Show me what you've got, Captain."

"Sir, these are satellite images of the location that have been taken over the last few hours." The first picture showed a very wide picture of some forest with a river running through it. "We believe this matches the description provided by the first hostages to be released. We've been gradually drilling down on various sections within the area and we discovered this." He showed the General a more detailed photo that seemed to show a tent hidden within the forest.

The General picked up the photo and held it close to his face trying to see the details. "It's hard to make it out. What's this up in the corner of the picture? Can you drill down and get me a better picture of what this is?"

"Already done sir," the Captain said as he showed the General the next picture. It was clearly a man dressed in camouflage and holding a rifle. "We've identified two separate gunmen in the photos. They appear to be guarding the occupants inside that tent."

"I think you may have found where these bastards have been hiding," the General said. "How long until we can deploy the fire team to that area?"

"They are already making their way through the forest, sir. I expect them to be at that location within half an hour. Permission requested to use force if necessary, sir?"

"Granted," the General said. The Captain spoke into his headset and relayed the approval to proceed using force to his marines on the ground. "Put them on the speaker when they get there," the General said. "I want to monitor this operation."

"Yes sir," the Captain replied.

Down in the forest, the four marines in the fire team moved through the rainforest with the quietness and precision of well-trained soldiers. It was about twenty minutes later when the fire team leader reported. "Braz Team 3 reporting. Target acquired. Three hostiles confirmed. Unknown personnel under cover. Permission to engage requested."

The Captain looked at the General who nodded his head. "Permission to engage granted," the Captain said.

Although the operation was now on speaker in the control room, there were hardly any other verbal communications broadcast. The fire team leader communicated with the rest of his team through a series of hand gestures. He signaled for the other marines to spread out so they would each be approaching from a different angle and they silently moved into position.

Suddenly the sound of a single shot exploded over the speaker in the control room. Two more quick gunshots followed shortly after and the General could hear the sound of the team leader and the rest of his team as they ran toward the tent. Everything went silent for several seconds, but then the speaker came alive with the sounds of a full-scale assault. This went on for about thirty seconds followed by a deathly silence. The only sound they could hear after that was the sound of the footsteps of the team leader as he crept through the compound. Everyone in the control room held their breath and it seemed to take forever for the team leader to report.

"Braz Team 3 reporting. Operation complete. Six hostiles KIA."

The General grabbed the headset from the Captain. "What about the hostages? Did you rescue the hostages?"

"That's a negative," the fire team leader reported. "No hostages found. The location appears to have been some kind of a drug distribution site. There's no indication that the hostages have ever been here."

"Damn it," the General yelled as he fired the headset across the room.

* * *

Back at the compound, the hostages all froze in fear when they heard the gunfire. It sounded like it originated only a few kilometres from where they were being held. Their guards were also spooked by what they heard. Eric could hear them arguing but he had no idea what they were saying. Maria understood their conversation and came over and sat beside Eric.

"We're running out of time," Maria whispered to him. "They've already been paid ten million dollars for the release of the hostages so far. Some of the guards don't want to wait any longer. They want to just kill the rest of us and make a run for it. But the doctor told them to wait for the final deadline."

"The final deadline?" Eric asked.

"Two days from now," Maria said.

* * *

"Hi Tom," Brian said into the phone. "I need you to transfer two million dollars to the following offshore account." Detective Mitchell pushed the piece of paper that had the account transit number in front of Brian and he read off the numbers to Tom. Now that some of the hostages had been released alive, Detective Mitchell had authorized the payment of additional ransoms.

"The money will be there in a matter of seconds," Tom said after he had read back the account number back to Brian for confirmation. "Is there anything else you need from me?"

"No," Brian replied. "Hopefully the boys will be released once they get the money."

"Melanie," Tom shouted after he got off the phone with Brian. "I need you to transfer two million dollars from our trust fund to the following offshore account number." He walked out of his office and handed Melanie the piece of paper with the account transit number.

Melanie started to enter the information into her computer with Tom looking over her shoulder. Melanie felt quite nervous. "What's going on?" she finally asked her boss, looking up at him fearing the answer.

Tom knew she deserved an explanation. "Brian Baxter's two sons have been kidnapped in Brazil," he said. "The two million dollars is to pay the ransom for their release."

"Oh my God!" Melanie said. She had been worried that her boss was somehow involved in some shady financial

139

scheme but this was far worse than what she could have ever imagined. She clicked the last button on her screen which transferred the money. A few seconds later, she received confirmation that the transaction had been completed. "Done," she said.

Tom headed back into his office and stared out of the window. He remembered when Brian and Jean had brought the two boys out to their cottage in Muskoka. Tom and his late wife, Betty, had never been able to have kids of their own so they had always treasured the days when the Baxters came out to visit them at the cottage. Brian and Jean would try to get some time away by themselves and Tom and his wife were always grateful that they could adopt the two boys, even if it was only for a weekend.

Tom remembered the first time he took Eric out in the boat and he had caught his first fish. They were going to eat it that night for supper but Eric wanted to save it until he could show his prize catch to his father. Tom looked down at the picture that was displayed on the credenza in his office showing Brian and Eric with the fish. Beside it was a picture of Chip flying into the lake after he had swung out on a rope that hung from a tree along the shore. Chip was more of a challenge for Tom and his wife to take care of because Chip had no fear. He would climb the highest tree or jump into the lake off of the highest rock.

Jean and Betty had also shared a special bond, as they had both been raised in Saskatchewan. They used to talk endlessly about the prairie sky and how the sky there was bigger and bluer than anywhere else in the world. And the two of them would plot how they were going to convince their husbands to move back to Saskatchewan when they retired.

"When will we know if the boys are safe?" Melanie asked

as she stood in the door of Tom's office.

Tom wiped his eyes as he was brought back from his daydream into the grim reality. "I don't know," he said.

* * *

Back in the room at FBI headquarters, Hilary Davis pleaded with her husband over the phone to just pay the ransom to get their two kids back. "You had your chance to rescue them, but you failed. It's now time to just pay the ransom."

"We're close, I know we are," General Davis replied. "We've still got two days until the final deadline. Just give me one more day to rescue them. If we don't find them within the next twenty four hours, I'll pay the ransom."

Brian couldn't hear what the General had said to his ex-wife over the phone, but the expression on her face told him that she hadn't convinced him to pay the ransom.

Over in the corner, Brian saw Detective Johnson sitting with Jamie Taylor and his sister Sarah. "We've both remortgaged our houses," Jamie said, "but we've only got a little over six hundred thousand dollars. Do you think they'd release our parents if we sent it to them?"

Detective Johnson shook his head. "The kidnappers have been very clear that they want a million dollars for each hostage."

"But it's everything we've got," Sarah cried.

"Do your parents have any life insurance policies they could cash in?" Detective Johnson asked. "Do you think the bank would give you an unsecured loan for the rest? I'll talk to your bank manager if you think it would help." The detective was trying anything he could think of to help them come up with more money.

Brian noticed Elizabeth Noble sitting at the back of the room crying. She was alone. "My husband refused to pay the ransom," she said to Brian when he sat down in the chair beside her. "He's got the money, but he just put on his coat and left. What kind of a father would do that?"

Brian didn't know what to say. As she started to cry again, Brian put his arm around her to try to comfort her. "I think all we can do now is just pray," he said.

*** CHAPTER 25 ***

The military-style truck exited from the trail that led deep into the forest where the prison compound was located and onto a more travelled road, although it was a road that was rarely used as well. The guards were taking Michael, the two Australians and the four Japanese men to a different drop-off point than the one they had used when they released the German hostages. They didn't want the police to be able to track them to where the rest of the hostages were being held.

In the distance, the guard driving the truck could see another vehicle approaching. They were not expecting to encounter any other vehicles on this trip. Not taking any chances, he turned off the road and down another small trail that led into the forest. He drove far enough into the forest so that their truck was not visible from the road, hoping that the people in the other vehicle had not even seen them and would simply continue on to wherever they were headed. He stopped the truck and then started walking back toward the main road to check, taking his rifle with him.

He hid under cover of the forest as he watched the vehicle on the main road approach. "Merda!" he cursed to himself as he watched the vehicle slow down. It was a Brazilian police vehicle. They were probably just doing a routine patrol looking for drug runners. The vehicle continued slowly by the place where they had turned into the forest and the guard thought they were going to get lucky. But when the police vehicle started to back up and then turned down the same trail where they had entered, he knew he was going to have to take action. He moved behind a tree as he watched the police vehicle slowly approach. When it was about twenty paces in front of him, he fired his rifle and the driver slumped over in his seat. But the other police officer threw open his car door and started returning fire using his door as a shield.

Upon hearing the gunfire, the guard that had been watching the hostages jumped out of the truck and ran down the trail to help his partner. Michael took advantage of this opportunity and threw off his hood and started untying the ropes that held them all together. Once he had his hands free, he started to untie the others. They could hear the gunfire taking place just down the trail. Suddenly, everything went silent.

Michael had no idea who had won the gunfight, but he didn't want to take any chances and wait around to find out. "I'd suggest we split up and make a run for it," he said to the other prisoners.

The two Australians leapt from the truck and started running through the forest as fast as they could. Michael untied two of the Japanese men and then told them to untie the other two.

Suddenly a shot ricocheted off of the cab of the truck. Michael ducked down behind the truck and took off through the forest running in a zig-zag pattern away the gunman, making it harder for him to line up his target. Michael heard some of the other hostages running as well but he wasn't going to wait for anyone this time. He had made that mistake with Greg and he wasn't going to make it again. It was every man for himself now. He ran for several kilometres before he stopped. He listened intently for any kind of sound, but heard nothing. He didn't move for several more minutes, but still heard nothing. He had escaped. He was free. "But where the hell am I?" he said to himself.

* * *

The doctor came walking into the compound and headed over to where Eric was sitting. "The ransom has been paid for you and your brother," the doctor said.

Eric walked over to where Chip was sitting and helped him to his feet. Although the infection was gone and his leg was much better, it was still not a hundred percent. The brothers just stood there hugging each other for what seemed like an eternity.

"What about the others?" Eric asked the doctor.

"The ransoms were only paid for you and your brother," the doctor replied. "Hopefully they'll pay the ransoms for the others before the final deadline."

Maria felt a tear starting to well up in her eye. She knew that she was just a poor girl from the favela and there would never be a ransom paid for her. She wandered away from the group over to the other side of the compound, but Eric followed her.

"I'm so happy for you and your brother," Maria said to Eric when he approached.

"We'd all be dead already if it wasn't for you," Eric said as he hugged her. "Don't give up hope. I'll do everything I can once we're free to come back to rescue you. And don't forget that Jacob and Emily's father is a marine and is probably already on his way to rescue everyone."

"Time to go," the doctor said. "We've got quite a hike ahead of us. The other guards haven't returned yet so I'll be leading you out of the forest myself."

The remaining hostages watched as the doctor tied Eric and Chip's hands together with about ten feet of rope and placed the hoods over their heads. But they were only about a hundred metres out of the camp when the doctor told them to stop. "I don't think we really need these," he said as he removed their hoods. They walked for several kilometres through the forest without saying a word. Eric was deep in thought about the people being left behind, particularly Maria because he doubted anyone would pay her ransom. They continued to walk through the dense forest until they came upon a jeep that was parked beside a deserted trail. This was a much smaller vehicle than the military-style truck that had been used in the kidnapping.

"You drive," the doctor said to Eric as he untied them. He told Chip to sit in the front seat and the doctor climbed into the back of the jeep where he could keep an eye on them with his rifle at the ready if they tried anything.

Eric paused before he started up the jeep. "What's going to happen to the others?" Eric asked.

"I think you know exactly what's going to happen to them," the doctor answered. And he was right. Eric did know.

"What if we got our father to pay more ransom money?" Eric asked.

"Are you sure you want to do that for a woman you barely know?" the doctor asked. He was well aware that Eric and Maria had become quite close during their ordeal. "Do you think your father is going to pay another million dollars for someone that's not family or that he's never even met?"

"Not one million dollars," Eric said. "How about another six and a half million for the release of all of the remaining hostages?"

Chip looked at his brother in amazement. "That's everything that dad has!" Chip said. "And you know he said that leaving a legacy was the most important thing to him."

"I know exactly what dad said and how much money he has," Eric said to his brother. "But we can't just leave them there to die. I think dad would agree."

Eric turned to look at the doctor. "Will you release the rest of the prisoners if my dad agrees to pay another six and a half million dollars?" The doctor could see the desperation in Eric's eyes.

"That's not up to me," the doctor replied. He thought for a few more seconds, then reached inside the backpack that he had brought with him and pulled out a satellite phone. He spoke on the phone for only a few seconds. "Tell him to call me, it's important," was all the doctor said before he disconnected.

"What now?" Eric asked.

"We wait," the doctor said.

They sat in the jeep in silence for over ten minutes before Chip spoke. "Thanks for stitching up my leg," he said. "I don't think I ever thanked you before." The doctor didn't respond. He knew that it was a mistake to build any kind of a relationship with the hostages, something he was finding more and more difficult the more he got to know them.

"How's your gout?" the doctor asked Eric after another silence of several minutes.

"Not so good," Eric replied. "That walk through the forest didn't do my ankle much good."

The doctor climbed out of the back of the jeep and started pulling some leaves off of one of the bushes that surrounded their jeep. "If you eat these leaves, your gout will be gone within twenty four hours," the doctor said.

"You're kidding," Eric said. "I'm not sure I should be eating stuff you picked off a bush."

"Suit yourself," the doctor said. "But there's a lot of medicines that are based on plants found in the rainforest."

Eric looked at the leaves considering what the doctor had just told him. He took a small bite out of one of the leaves. It actually didn't taste that bad, sort of like spinach.

"You don't seem like your typical kidnapper," Eric said. "I mean, you went to medical school at UCLA and you're obviously a good doctor. How did you become a kidnapper?"

"I'm not one of the kidnappers," the doctor said.

"Could have fooled me," Eric said. "You're the one with the gun."

"My family just asked for my help when they thought Chip here was going to die," the doctor said. "You don't get any ransom money for a dead guy."

"Sounds like you've got a hell of a family," Eric said.

"That's why they kicked me out of the United States. When I applied for a work visa as a doctor after I graduated UCLA, they discovered my family's criminal past. Even though I stayed clear of all of that stuff, they painted me with the same brush and deported me back to Brazil. My brother was also living in the States at the time running a successful business, but they deported him as well. When he got back to Brazil, he decided to join the family business."

"So your family's in the kidnapping business?" Chip asked.

"They'll do whatever makes them the most money.

Twenty years ago, my dad and his brothers used to run guns through Columbia, then they used to sell drugs here in Brazil. But when they started cracking down on the drug trade here before the World Cup and the Olympics, the family decided they'd get out of the drug business and into the kidnapping business."

Suddenly the satellite phone lit up and the doctor answered the call. "What's wrong?" said the voice on the phone. It was the doctor's brother.

"I've got the two Baxter boys with me right now," the doctor said.

"Their ransom has been paid," his brother said. "They can be released."

"I know," the doctor said, "but they want to know if we'll release the rest of the hostages if they can get their father to pay another six and a half million dollars."

"Are they sure he'll pay?"

The doctor looked at both Eric and Chip. He could tell that they hoped he would, but weren't really sure. "They think he will.," the doctor said.

"I don't like it," his brother said. "It could just be a trick to give the police more time to find our location."

Suddenly another voice was heard on the call. "I'm confident Mr. Baxter will pay more money. I think we should do it. But don't have him transfer the money to the account given to the police. Have him transfer the money to this account." The mysterious caller gave the transit number for a different account number which was written down by the doctor.

"Okay, but I still don't like it," his brother said. "If the father doesn't pay the additional money, kill them all – including his two sons."

The satellite phone suddenly went dead. "What happened?" Eric asked.

"I ended the call," the doctor said. "Your time was up. We have to limit each call to less than a minute to prevent them from tracking our location."

"But I still have to call my father," Eric said.

"I know," the doctor said, "but we're going to change locations before you make that call. Start the jeep." The doctor made Eric drive the jeep a few kilometres turning down paths that didn't seem wide enough for a person, let alone a jeep. "Stop here," the doctor said.

The doctor started to hand Eric the satellite phone, but then held onto it for a few seconds more. "Are you sure you want to do this? One thing to think about is that the guards back at the compound were getting pretty nervous. They may have already killed the rest of the hostages and made a run for it."

Eric already knew that the guards had talked about killing them by what Maria had told him. "We have to try," Eric said.

"It's your life," the doctor said releasing his hold on the phone.

*** CHAPTER 26 ***

Brian was lying on the leather bench in the hallway at FBI headquarters staring out the window and watching the clouds roll by. The hallway and the window had become his own little private sanctuary during the ordeal.

"We need everyone back in the meeting room," Detective Johnson said. "The Brazilian police have some new information to report." When Brian entered the room, he could see the various TV screens already lit up with the participants from the various countries.

"We've recovered a few more of the hostages," the Brazilian police officer reported. Brian noted that the officer had used the word *recovered* rather than *rescued* and his heart sank. "Two of our officers encountered the kidnappers and some of the hostages while on a regular patrol through the region. Both of our officers and one of the kidnappers were killed in the ensuing gunfight."

"What about the hostages?" Detective Mitchell asked.

"Two of the Japanese hostages were later found wandering through the forest, shaken, but unharmed. Unfortunately, we also found the bodies of the two other

Japanese hostages a short distance from the site of the encounter. They had both been executed." The Brazilian policeman gave the names of the two Japanese hostages that had been found alive and the names of the two hostages who had not been so lucky.

"Based on interviews we conducted with the two Japanese hostages that we rescued, we believe Michael Porter and Oliver and Lucas Williams escaped into the forest during the gunfight. We are continuing to search for them."

"What about Eric and Chip Baxter?" Brian asked.

The Brazilian police officer leaned over and asked one of the Japanese men who was sitting beside him. "They were not part of this group of hostages," the policeman reported.

Brian knew that he had paid the ransom for his two sons later than the ransoms had been paid for the Australians and the Japanese hostages. He didn't know if that was a good thing or not. On one hand, his sons might still be released unharmed. But he was also worried that the kidnappers might just kill all of the remaining hostages. After the update was completed, Brian wandered back out into the hallway to his sanctuary. He laid down on the leather bench underneath the window in the hallway watching the clouds roll by until he fell asleep.

"Thank you for paying the ransom for the boys," Jean said to Brian in his dream.

"I probably should have paid it sooner," Brian said. "I hope I didn't wait too long."

"It's not your fault. You were just following the advice of Detective Mitchell."

"Yeah I know, but I'm still worried that I may have left it too late. I'm glad Detective Johnson told me he would pay the ransom if it was for a member of his own family."

"If you had paid the ransom earlier, the boys might have

been killed like those Japanese hostages," Jean tried to reassure him.

"I suppose you're right," Brian replied. "I just hope that they're still alive."

"They are," Jean said. "I can feel it in my soul." She hated to see her husband suffering through this ordeal. "Answer your phone," she said.

"What?" Brian asked.

"Answer your phone," Jean said again. "It's Eric."

Brian bolted up from his sleep when he realized his cell phone was ringing. He quickly pulled it out of his pocket. The display indicated it was an unknown caller. "Eric?" Brian said hopefully.

"Yeah, it's me," Eric replied.

"Are you okay?" Brian asked. Before he had a chance to answer, Brian asked several more questions. "Is Chip alright? Where are you? Can I come and get you? You sound like you're calling from the moon."

"Chip and I are okay," Eric said. "I'm calling from the middle of the rainforest." Eric paused trying to figure out how to ask the next question. "Dad, can you send six and a half million dollars to pay the ransoms for the rest of the hostages?"

Brian was confused. "I already paid two million dollars ransom for you and your brother. Are you saying they now want another six and a half million for your release?"

"No, the extra money is for the rest of the hostages," Eric said. "They're going to kill them unless you send the money." Eric didn't have the heart to tell his father that they'd put themselves back in danger and that they'd also be killed if they didn't get the money. He gave his father the account transit number to be used to send the money. "Don't tell the FBI about this account," Eric warned.

Brian wondered if Eric was being forced by the

kidnappers to ask for more money with a gun held to his head. "Can we trust them? How do we know they're not just going to keep asking for more money?" Brian didn't know what to do. "Just tell me what to do son."

"Send the money dad." The doctor grabbed the phone from Eric and ended the call before Brian had a chance to ask any more questions.

* * *

Brian sat on the leather bench trying to calm himself. His heart was pounding and he felt a tightness in his chest that was making it difficult for him to catch his breath. He knew he should go tell Detective Mitchell about the call, but he was afraid – afraid that he would talk him out of paying the additional ransom. He thought for a few more minutes, but then hit the numbers on his phone to call Tom Beamish. Tom had been sitting by his phone for the last few days waiting to hear if the boys had been released.

"Are the boys okay?" Tom asked when he saw who was calling.

"Tom, I need another six and a half million dollars," Brian said.

"Do you need it wired to the same account as before?"

"No, they've given me another account number," Brian said. He read off the transit number to Tom. "Send the money as soon as you can."

Brian hung up the phone and saw Detective Johnson standing in the doorway of the meeting room. Brian didn't know how much of the previous telephone conversations the detective had overheard. "I had to," Brian said. "I know we're supposed to put everything through you guys first, but I couldn't take any chances."

Detective Johnson came over and sat down beside Brian. "I understand," the detective said. "You gotta do what you gotta do when it's your family."

After he hung up the phone, Tom Beamish was searching his brain trying to figure out how he was going to come up with another six and a half million dollars to wire to the kidnappers. Sure, Eric had that much money sitting in his investments, but it was too late in the day to have those investments cashed out to be used. "Melanie, how much money is sitting in the trust fund?" he yelled to his assistant.

"We've got a little over two million of Mr. McKenzie's money sitting in there waiting to be invested," Melanie replied. "And we've got about another million of Mr. Ronson's money sitting there waiting for his real estate deal to close. Why?" She came and stood in the doorway of Tom's office and knew something was wrong by the look she saw on her boss's face.

"It's probably best if you not know what I'm about to do," Tom said to his assistant. "There's no point both of us going to jail."

Tom immediately picked up the phone as he was going to have to find another three and a half million dollars within a matter of minutes. It was time to call in some markers from some people who had access to that kind of money, no questions asked. "Hi Randy, it's Tom Beamish."

Randy had been Tom's first boss when he was getting started in the investment business. He had been running his own investment company for years and had been investigated for some shady investment practices several times, but nothing had ever stuck. However, several other people from his company had been involved in some investment scams and a few had gone to jail. Tom had worked for Randy for about a year and had learned a lot from him, but he had decided to leave because there were too many hush-hush meetings going on behind closed doors.

"Tom Beamish," Randy said. "Well, there's a voice from the past. What's it been, ten years since we last spoke?"

"At least," Tom answered. He hated making this call but he didn't know where else to turn. "I'm in a bit of a jam and I need your help. I need to get my hands on three and a half million dollars within the next hour."

Randy could not hide his shock at the request. He knew Tom always did everything above board and by the book. He knew Tom must have a good reason for making the request. "What's going on?"

Tom explained the situation about the kidnappings. "Those two boys are like my own sons so I have to get the money somehow. I can have the money back to you tomorrow when the markets open again."

There was an eerie silence on the other end of the phone as Tom waited for a response. But he could hear Randy hitting the keys on his keyboard. Finally, Randy responded. "Where do you want me to send the money?"

Tom gave a heavy sigh of relief. He gave Randy the details to transfer the funds to his trust account. Sure enough, the money appeared in the account a few minutes later.

Tom checked the balance in the trust account and saw that it was a little over the six and a half million he required. He hit the keys to transfer the money to the offshore account of the kidnappers and was relieved to see the confirmation that the transaction had been completed.

Tom knew that these transactions would trigger an STR. Suspicious Transaction Reports were how the authorities investigated potential money laundering transactions and he knew that he would soon be getting a visit from them to explain everything. Hopefully his explanation would avoid him serving any time in jail, but he knew a hefty fine would probably be levied. Still, it would all be worth it if it meant that Eric and Chip would be returned safely.

*** CHAPTER 27 ***

"For your sake, I hope he does send the money," the doctor said. "We should start our walk back to the compound before it gets too dark. I suggest you remember the way because you'll be walking this route on your own if he comes through with the money."

The doctor put the satellite phone back into his backpack and pulled out a handgun. Both Eric and Chip held their breath in fear. "Do you know how to use a 9mm semi-automatic pistol?" the doctor casually asked.

"No," Eric said. "Why?"

"Because you might need to know to get yourself out of here alive if your father comes through with the ransom. This rainforest is crawling with drug runners, not to mention any wild animals you might encounter." The doctor quickly showed them how to load a magazine of bullets into the bottom of the gun. "Remember to keep your finger on the side of the gun and not on the trigger."

"So is it ready to fire now?" Eric asked.

"No, because there's no bullet in the chamber," the doctor said. He grasped the top of the gun and pulled it back. "That loads a bullet into the chamber and the gun is now hot."

"I've never held a gun in my life," Eric said. "I'd be afraid I'd shoot myself in the foot. Does it have a safety?"

The doctor showed Eric where the safety was on the gun. "That might be a good idea with this gun," the doctor said, "because this gun has been known to accidently discharge without pulling the trigger. The Brazilian police just recalled over 90,000 of these guns and let's just say my family intercepted a few of them before they made it back to the manufacturer." The doctor unloaded the gun and pushed the magazine of bullets into the seat cushion. "I'm going to leave this pistol underneath the seat in the jeep for when you get back here, assuming you do."

The three of them started their walk back to the compound with Chip in the lead and the doctor holding the rifle and trailing behind them, giving directions to Chip about which way to go. Eric saw his brother periodically deliberately break a branch to mark their trail. The doctor saw him do it as well, but he didn't care. If the ransom was paid, he knew they'd have to walk out of the forest on their own. If the ransom wasn't paid, they wouldn't be walking anywhere.

Maria was staring mindlessly out through the wire fence surrounding their compound when she saw the shadows of three men walking out of the forest. She assumed it was the other guards returning. "Eric," she shouted when she recognized who it was. She was torn with mixed emotions. On one hand, she was glad to see him again as she was sure he had walked out of her life forever when he had left. But she was also frightened at seeing him being led back into their prison. She ran to hug him as he came through the opening in the wire fence.

"Hi Maria," Eric said, hugging her back. "See, I told you

I'd be back."

"What's going on?" Maria asked. The Girards, the Taylors and Jacob and Emily Davis also came over to hear why they'd returned.

"Chip and I asked our father to pay the ransom for the release of all of the hostages," Eric said.

"And he agreed?" Maria asked.

"I think so," Eric said. "We got cut off, but I'm pretty sure he'll come through."

Maria was overwhelmed. She couldn't imagine anyone paying a ransom for her, let alone someone she'd never even met.

As the night wore on, they all lay on the ground listening to the sounds of the forest and wondering what their fate would be in the morning. Jacob and Emily Davis continued to peer out into the darkness wondering if and when the marines would come swooping in to rescue them, but even Jacob was starting to have his doubts. The Girards laid huddled together filled with renewed optimism that they might actually get to see their kids again. The Taylors also huddled together, but the ordeal seemed to be taking an increasing toll on them. Eric wondered if they'd have the strength to walk out of the rainforest when their ransoms were paid.

Maria came over and was hovering around where Eric and Chip were laying, but not saying a word. "I think she wants to spend some quality time with one of us," Chip said, "and I don't think it's me." Chip got up and headed over to the other side of the compound.

"Something on your mind?" Eric said to Maria. Maria didn't respond but just laid down beside him giving him a full embrace which was returned with equal fervor by Eric.

"I can't believe your father would pay the ransom for people he doesn't even know," Maria whispered to Eric.

"Does he have that much money?"

"Yeah, but it's everything he's got," Eric whispered back. "It's his entire legacy."

"Why would he do that?"

"Because Chip and I asked him to," Eric said. "But once we're free, I'm going to spend the rest of my life trying to pay him back."

"How are you going to do that?" Maria asked.

"I have no idea," Eric said, "but I'll figure out a way."

Maria had no doubt that he would. "Tell me about your family."

"What would you like to know?"

"Everything," Maria said, giving him a squeeze. "Don't leave anything out."

"Well, you already know Chip. He's my only sibling. We're from a mid-sized city in Canada called London. Do you know anything about Canada?"

"Practically nothing," Maria said, "other than I hear it's cold up there."

"Yeah, it is in the winter but our summers can get quite hot, although not as hot as it is in this rainforest. Chip moved to the U.S. to go to school and became a U.S. citizen, which is why he competed for the U.S. in the Olympics. He's always been a good athlete and my mom and dad and I spent a lot of time travelling to watch him compete in various competitions. We had a lot of fun on those trips." Eric paused before continuing. "I wish my mom was still alive to see him compete in the Olympics. She would have been so proud of him."

"What happened to your mom?" Maria asked.

"She died of cancer about five years ago. We all miss her but I know my dad finds it really hard. He used to talk about how much he was looking forward to their retirement years, but that all got cut short. We used to have big parties on my mom's birthday. In fact, my dad still has a family dinner every year on her birthday."

"I've never been to a birthday party in my whole life," Maria confessed.

"Well, you're officially invited to my mom's next birthday party," Eric said. "So tell me about your family."

"There's not much to tell," Maria said. "I already told you my dad was a drug dealer and a gang leader, but he was killed."

"So you and your mom just take care of each other now?" Eric asked.

Maria couldn't remember the last time her mother had taken care of her. "Let's just say we live in the same place." Maria didn't want to talk any more about herself. She much preferred to hear about Eric and his family. "Tell me more about your family."

Eric spent the next few hours telling Maria stories about the times with their aunts, uncles and cousins out at the lake in Saskatchewan. He told her how his mother loved to sing and how she used to send out musical newsletters at Christmas with updates about the family. Being part of such a family was a foreign concept to Maria, but she loved to hear Eric talk about it.

Eventually, they both drifted off to sleep. This was the first time since they'd been kidnapped that Eric didn't sleep with one eye open.

*** CHAPTER 28 ***

"General Davis," Captain Walmsley said into the phone. "We believe we may have found the location where the hostages are being held."

"Are you sure it's not just another drug operation site?" the General scolded.

The Captain was not about to make the same mistake again. He had been scouring over the satellite images ever since his first mistake. He had a huge map showing the location where the first German hostages had been found and the location where the Brazilian police had found the bodies of the two Japanese hostages that had been killed. He figured the latter location would be pretty close to the site where the hostages were being held because the kidnappers had been intercepted in their route to their planned drop-off point. Using that as a reference point, he had found another location on the satellite pictures that showed a tent hidden in the forest that was close to a river. Ironically, it was only a few kilometres from the first location he had found. But the clinching piece of evidence were the three brief satellite calls that they had detected that had been placed within the last few hours from the middle of the rainforest. All of the calls were placed from less than two kilometres of the new target location. "I'm confident that this is the correct location sir. I can have the fire team deployed to that site at day break. Permission to proceed requested sir."

"Approved," the General said.

* * *

Oliver and Lucas Williams continued their journey through the rainforest. When the gunfight had started between the guards and the Brazilian patrol officers, they had raced through the forest as fast as they could trying to get away from the kidnappers. At one point they had seen Michael running through the forest and they had tried to follow him, but he was much too fast for them to keep up. Now they were just wandering through the forest as they had no idea which direction to head. To make matters worse, it was starting to get dark.

"We should try to find a place to camp for the night," Lucas said.

"You're probably right," Oliver answered, "but I'm not sure I'll be able to sleep. Who knows what kind of animals roam through the forest here at night."

Lucas hadn't even thought about that, but now that his brother had told him, he was finding it hard to think about anything else. Suddenly, getting away from the kidnappers seemed less of a concern than avoiding getting attacked by some wild animal while they slept. "We should probably take turns sleeping while the other one keeps watch," Lucas said. Lucas agreed to take the first watch.

"Do you think they have bears or cougars in this forest?" Oliver asked. It was obvious he was going to have trouble sleeping.

"I don't think there are any bears in Brazil," Lucas replied. "And I think they have jaguars instead of cougars, but I'm not sure."

"You're not helping," Oliver said.

"You asked," his brother replied. Lucas decided it was best that he not tell his brother about the snakes that could also be found in the rainforest. "Don't worry about it. I'll keep watch while you sleep." Still, it took Oliver over an hour until he finally fell asleep. Unfortunately, Lucas drifted off shortly thereafter as well.

The sun was just coming up when they were both awakened by a rustling in the forest. They both looked at each other, frozen in fear. They had no weapons to defend themselves from a predator. They remained completely still and silent hoping that whatever was moving through the forest would simply pass them by, but it was probably following their scent as it seemed to be coming directly toward them.

Whatever it was seemed to be climbing a tree about twenty paces from where Lucas and Oliver were huddled in fear. Or more accurately, trying to climb a tree. "Shit," they heard someone yell.

"Michael?" Lucas yelled when he recognized the voice.

They heard a big crash as Michael fell out of the tree and landed in some bushes below it. Michael winced in pain as the bruises from his beating were still pretty fresh. Lucas and Oliver went running over to see if he was alright. "Good to see you mate," Oliver said.

"What are you trying to do?" Lucas asked as he helped Michael out of the bush.

Michael had knocked the wind out of himself so it took him a few minutes until he could answer. "I've been wandering through the bush trying to figure out which way to go when I remembered that Maria said to head toward

Pico da Tijuca. She said it's the highest point around here and I should be able to see it from anywhere, so I was trying to climb a tree to see if I could see it."

"Here, let Lucas give it a go," Oliver said. "He's half monkey."

Lucas climbed on Oliver's shoulders with Michael holding him steady. Lucas managed to grab a branch and pull himself up into the tree. After that, he quickly climbed the tree moving from branch to branch with ease. "See, I told you he could climb like a monkey," Oliver said.

"Can you see the mountain?" Michael shouted.

"Yes, it's that direction," Lucas yelled while pointing in the direction they should head. "But it's quite a few kilometres away."

"Yeah, but at least we now know what direction to head," Michael said. When Lucas reached the ground again, the three of them started on their journey to freedom.

*** CHAPTER 29 ***

Maria nudged Eric's shoulder as he slept beside her. "Something's wrong," Maria said.

Eric raised his head and gazed around the compound. Although the sun was barely up, he could see well enough to make everything out. "I don't see anything," he whispered back to Maria.

"Exactly," Maria said. "There's no one guarding the entrance to the compound."

Eric got to his feet and started to walk toward the entrance, but still couldn't see anyone. Perhaps the guard had fallen asleep or had just headed off to relieve himself. "Hello?" Eric shouted. There was no response.

The other hostages in the compound started to stir when they heard Eric yell. "What's going on?" Chip asked as he walked toward his brother.

"I'm not sure," Eric replied. "There doesn't appear to be anyone guarding us. Hello, is anyone here?" Eric yelled, this time much louder than the first time. Again there was no response.

"Stay here," Eric said to his brother. "I'm going to go

check it out." Eric slowly stepped through the wire fence and headed over to where the guards would normally be sitting. "They're gone," Eric shouted back to everyone in the compound.

Slowly the rest of them came walking out of the compound to join Eric. "It appears that they all left sometime in the middle of the night," Eric said. "I guess Dad came through with the ransom."

"What do we do now?" Jean-Pierre asked.

"We find our way out of the forest and back to civilization," Eric said. They gathered up their few belongings and prepared to leave. Eric used the plastic first aid kit to get himself one final drink of water before their journey and suggested the others do the same. They weren't sure when they would next be able to get a drink as they had no way to carry water with them.

Suddenly, Eric saw the glint of something metal leaning up against a tree and headed over to check it out. He was pleased so see it was a steel water bottle.

"One of the guards must have left it behind by accident," Maria said.

When Eric saw the UCLA logo on the side of the water bottle, he knew it hadn't been left behind by mistake. The doctor had left it for them on purpose. Eric took it over to the water pail and filled it. He knew it could be quite a while until they got their next drink.

"I know the way," Chip said. The nine hostages began their trek out of the forest with Chip leading the group. Jacob and Emily Davis were next with the Girards falling in behind them. The Taylors followed them, but it was apparent that the journey out of the rainforest was going to be difficult on them. Eric and Maria were the last two in the group.

Chip was glad he had left the markings showing the way

out of the forest. Despite that, he paused several times confused about which direction to go. Periodically he would ask Eric if he knew which way to go, which he sometimes did. Other times, they were both unsure and they simply guessed. In some parts, it looked like the rainforest had grown another foot overnight and completely covered their tracks from the day before.

Eric and Maria were keeping an eye on Owen Taylor, worried that he would have another heart attack. Several times, Eric yelled to Chip to stop so that everyone could have a rest. He claimed it was because the gout in his ankle was bothering him, but those leaves that the doctor had told him to eat the day before had cured his gout almost completely. Eric was actually requesting the rest breaks so that the Taylors could catch their breath. He knew that Owen Taylor would not like to think that he was slowing them down.

With the numerous stoppages to rest, and several back-tracks after they realized they had gone the wrong way, it was taking them a lot longer to walk out of the forest than planned. With the sun now in full force, the temperature in the forest felt like it was about a million degrees. Everyone was pleased when they saw the jeep come into view.

When they reached the jeep, Eric reached under the driver's seat to find the handgun the doctor had left there for them. He also grabbed the magazine of bullets from the seat cushion loaded them into the handgun like the doctor has showed him. He cocked the gun making it "hot", using the expression the doctor had used. Even thinking about that caused Eric's heart to race so he engaged the external safety like the doctor had shown him. "We probably won't encounter any drug runners or wild animals," Eric thought, trying to reassure himself.

Chip climbed into the driver's seat of the jeep. Because

there wasn't enough room for all of them in the jeep, Eric suggested Owen Taylor sit in the passenger's seat with his wife sitting on his lap. The Girards climbed into the back of the jeep. Eric, Maria and the two Davis kids would walk along behind the jeep. "Hold on," Chip said as he started up the jeep. "This is going to be a bumpy ride."

Chip drove slowly through the forest trying to find the path of least resistance. Because the jeep was old and heavily loaded, it bottomed out several times sending a jar through everyone inside. Chip was trying to drive slowly but sometimes he had to gun the engine to give it enough power to make it through the brush. The people walking were going just as fast as the jeep was, but Eric was glad that the Taylors got to ride because he wasn't sure they would make it otherwise.

Up ahead they thought they could see a clearing and it looked like they were approaching a more major road. Chip gunned the engine to try to make it over a tree branch that had fallen in their path. When they all heard the clunk from underneath the jeep, they immediately knew that had been a mistake. Chip continued to push on the gas pedal but they weren't moving.

"Let's see if we can push it out of this mess," Eric said. Eric, Maria and the two Davis kids pushed as hard as they could but couldn't move the jeep. The Girards got out of the back of the jeep and Jean-Pierre tried to help push, but quickly realized his shoulder was in no shape to be putting any strain on it.

They continued to push from behind with Chip pushing on the gas pedal trying to rock it off of the tree branch. It wasn't working. "Hold on," Eric said. "Let me take a look." He peered underneath the jeep and quickly determined they weren't going to be going any further in the jeep. "The axle is broken," he said. "I guess we have to walk from here."

Everyone climbed out of the jeep and started walking toward the clearing up ahead. They were encouraged to see that it was a road. Not a major road, but enough to have two distinct tire tracks. "Which way do you think we should go?" Eric said as he stood in the middle of the road looking back in forth in both directions looking for a clue.

"This way," Maria said as she came to stand beside Eric. She pointed to Pico da Tijuca which could be seen clearly in the distance.

*** CHAPTER 30 ***

"Braz Team 3 reporting," the fire team leader said. "We've located the kidnap site."

"How many hostiles?" the Captain asked.

"None. It appears that they've left," the fire team leader said. "Waiting for confirmation." The team leader watched as the members of his squad cautiously approached the compound ready to shoot any hostiles they encountered. It was only a minute or so later when they signaled the all-clear sign back to their leader.

As the marines surveyed the compound site, they could see the footprints of multiple people and could easily see the path they had taken into the forest. The team leader saw the wooden water pail sitting in the middle of the compound. He could also see the water on the ground surrounding the water pail where Eric and the others had taken their last drinks before heading off on their journey. The wetness on the ground told him that they had been there no more than an hour earlier.

"No sign of the kidnappers or the hostages," the team leader reported to the Captain. "But they can't be too far away. We are beginning pursuit."

* * *

Up ahead, the hostages continued their trek along the road toward their freedom keeping Pico da Tijuca in their sites on the horizon. Chip led the way and was walking at a much quicker pace than the others. As he did so, he could start to feel the burning sensation in his leg where the stitches were. But the pain was bearable so he continued to push the pace. As he glanced back, he could see the others spread out in a line behind. For a few seconds, he flashed back to his 5,000 metre Olympic race. That race seemed like a lifetime ago even though it was only about a week earlier. He was aware of someone on his right side and he glanced over his shoulder, half expecting to see Michael go gliding by him to the finish line. But it wasn't Michael, it was Jean-Pierre. "I was wondering if you could slow the pace a bit," Jean-Pierre said. "We're having trouble keeping up."

"Sorry," Chip said.

"Okay everyone, let's take a break," Eric said when they had all caught up to where Chip was waiting. He could tell the Taylors desperately needed to take a break.

Anita Taylor was walking arm-in-arm with her husband helping him along. "Don't stop on my account," Owen Taylor said. The last thing he wanted to do was to slow them down.

But the sun above them now seemed to be at its strongest and even Eric was feeling the strain. He noticed a small clearing along the side of the road that would offer them some shade. "Let's rest in the shade for about twenty minutes," Eric said as he pointed out the location.

Eric pulled the water bottle with the UCLA logo out of his pocket. He knew the water inside would be pretty warm, but at least it was wet. He offered the water bottle to the Taylors first.

"Let everyone else take a drink first," Owen said. He refused to be a burden to the group.

Eric took a quick swig from the water bottle, but it was just enough to wet his lips. He passed the water bottle to the rest of them in turn who each took a sip. When Emily Davis passed the water bottle to her brother, he just passed it on to the next person.

"I'm good," Jacob said as he glanced at the Taylors. They had barely drank a third of the contents when Jacob took the water bottle back over to Owen Taylor. "Take as much as you need."

Owen Taylor drank a couple of mouthfuls and then passed the water bottle to his wife. She refused to drink any water until Jacob encouraged her. "It's important that you stay hydrated," he said.

As Eric watched Jacob, he knew that the General would be proud of his son. When Jacob passed the water bottle back to Eric, there was only about two good mouthfuls left. Eric knew that last bit of water would become more and more precious as they continued their journey.

"Do you think it would be best if I went ahead to look for help?" Chip whispered to his brother as they sat in the shade. He didn't want the Taylors to overhear their conversation.

Eric had been wondering the same thing. "No, I think it's probably best if we all stay together," he whispered back. "I'm surprised there hasn't been a single vehicle go down the road in the entire time we've been walking. Once the sun starts to go down, it should cool off a bit and it won't be so hard on the Taylors."

But having the sun go down would present them with another problem – the darkness and whatever predators there might be lurking in the forest. Eric felt the gun in his pocket and felt grateful that the doctor had left it for him.

"Okay, let's go," Eric said after they had rested for about half an hour. A few clouds were now blocking out the direct sunlight and Eric wondered whether there was a major storm coming.

They were now walking as a group again with Chip leading the way and Eric pulling up the rear. Chip would regularly look back to make sure that he wasn't going too fast for the others to keep up.

As they walked along the road, Eric had the eerie feeling that they were being watched. The doctor had warned him about some of the predators in the rainforest and he gripped the gun he was carrying in his pocket a little tighter.

Suddenly two men came running out of the bushes alongside the road with their rifles pointed straight at Eric. Eric raised his gun and pointed it directly at one of the men. He wondered if they could see the barrel of the gun shaking as much as he could. He pointed his gun at the second man and then back to the first, not knowing which one he should shoot first, if he could actually pull the trigger at all.

It was only at that point that Eric remembered that he still had the external safety on the gun engaged. He wouldn't be able to fire now even if he did find the courage.

Suddenly a shot was fired from the other side of the road and Eric fell to the ground. The shooter emerged from the forest with his rifle ready to fire again if necessary.

"Braz 3 team reporting," the fire team leader said. "One hostile neutralized. Hostages recovered safely."

"Eric," Maria screamed as she rushed over to where he had fallen. She could already see the red blood stain growing on Eric's shirt, on the left side of his chest just below the collar bone. She cradled his head and covered his body with hers. If they were going to try to shoot him again, the bullet would have to go through her to get to him.

Chip came running back down the road to where his brother lay, ignoring the commands of the marine who had fired the shot. The rest of the hostages stood like stones with their hands held in the air.

"Cease fire!" the fire team commander screamed. He was quickly coming to realize that they had shot one of the hostages and not one of the kidnappers. However, the marine who had fired the shot did not lower his rifle until he kicked the handgun away from where it lay beside Eric.

"Braz Team 3 reporting," the fire team leader said. "Immediate medical assistance required. Location is 22 degrees, 54 minutes south, 43 degrees, 12 minutes west. Immediate medical assistance required."

Jacob Davis had been around marines his entire life so he knew they were U.S. Marines and that this team had probably been sent by his father. "Why did you shoot him?" he asked the marine who had fired the shot. "He's not one of the kidnappers. He's one of the hostages."

The marine did not respond but the look on his face couldn't hide the guilt he felt inside. One of the other marines pulled him aside as the team leader knelt beside Eric and applied pressure to his wound.

About a kilometer further ahead on the road, Michael and the two Australians froze in their tracks when they heard the gunshot. They wondered if the kidnappers were still tracking them so they hid in the forest alongside the road.

"What do you think we should do?" Lucas asked.

"I don't know," Michael said. They continued to hide in the bushes alongside the road as they thought.

"I think we should hide further back in the forest," Oliver said after a few minutes. "But we have to make sure we don't leave a trail that they can follow." The three of them slowly navigated their way farther away from the road, making sure they didn't break any branches or leave any sign of a trail.

It was about ten minutes later when they heard the sound of sirens and saw two Brazilian police vehicles go screaming by their location. An ambulance went racing by a few seconds after that. They now wished they had just waited alongside the road so the police would have seen them. They sprinted back toward the road, but the emergency vehicles were already gone. As they peered out of the forest, they could see the flashing lights of the emergency vehicles down the road.

"We should head toward those flashing lights," Michael said as he led them out of the cover of the forest. "They'll be able to help us." As they walked toward the vehicles, they could gradually start to make out the people standing in the road. When Michael recognized Chip, he broke into a full sprint.

"What happened?" Michael asked as he came running up.

"It's Eric," Chip said. "He's been shot."

"Is he going to make it?" Michael asked as he watched the paramedics load Eric into the back of the ambulance.

The paramedic didn't really answer the question. "He's lost a lot of blood," was all that he said.

*** CHAPTER 31 ***

"We have an update from Brazil," Detective Mitchell shouted trying to get everyone to convene back in the meeting room.

When Brian walked into the room, he could already see the TV monitors coming to life showing the feeds from the other locations. The feed from Brazil showed the head of the Brazilian police at the microphone but it also showed a few of the hostages in the background.

"Sylvia," Elizabeth Noble sighed in relief as she saw her daughter on the TV screen. "Thank God you're still alive."

"We'd like to report that we've found the hostages," the Brazilian police chief said. The TV camera then panned to show each of their faces. Jamie and Sarah felt grateful when they saw their parents, the Taylors, appear on the TV screen, although they were concerned that their father was sitting in a wheelchair with heart monitors on his chest and an IV in his arm. Hilary Davis was relieved when she saw Jacob and Emily standing behind the Taylors. Kevin and Lisa Porter hugged each other and shuddered in relief when they saw their son Michael.

"Thank you for paying the ransom for our parents," Jamie Taylor said to Brian, but he wasn't sure Brian was listening.

Even though he wasn't a religious man, Brian held his hands in prayer waiting to see the faces of his sons appear on the screen. He thought his prayers had been answered when he saw Chip standing beside Michael. But then the camera stopped moving.

"Unfortunately, one of the hostages was shot during the rescue attempt," the police chief said. Brian didn't have to wait to hear who had been shot. He felt the life drain from his body. "Eric Baxter is currently in surgery in critical condition," the police chief continued. "We will give further updates as they become available."

Suddenly General Davis came racing into the room and headed immediately over to Brian. "I'm so sorry," the General said.

"What have you done?" Hilary Davis asked.

The General looked at her briefly, but then turned his focus back to Brian. "I have a jet waiting to fly you to Rio," he said. The General helped Brian gather his things to get ready to leave.

Elizabeth Noble came over and gave Brian a hug. "Thank you so much for saving my Sylvia," she said. "I hope your son will be alright." But Brian didn't really hear her as he'd almost gone completely numb. He didn't remember racing through the streets of Houston in the General's car on the way to the airport, nor boarding the plane that the General had commandeered to fly them to Rio. He just stared blindly out of the window during the entire flight.

* * *

"Mr. Baxter," the General said several hours later as they

179

were beginning their descent into Rio. But Brian didn't hear him. "Mr. Baxter," the General said again, this time touching him on his arm. Brian came out of his trance just as the huge "Christ the Redeemer" statue came into view through the window of the plane. He remembered pointing it out to Eric as they had flown into Rio together only days earlier. "Mr. Baxter," the General continued. "I've just received word that your son is out of surgery. They think he's going to make it."

When Brian made it to the hospital in Rio, he found Chip sitting in the waiting room along with Michael. He gave Chip an enormous hug holding onto him for what seemed like an eternity. "How is Eric doing?" he asked.

"He's out of surgery but still in intensive care," Chip said. "He's still unconscious and they haven't let us in to see him yet, but the doctor said he may have got lucky as the bullet went clean through him. But he lost a lot of blood, so they're not sure."

Chip helped his father sit down in the chair beside him and Brian rocked back and forth with his hands held in prayer in front of him. As he swayed back and forth, he noticed a trickle of blood down Chip's leg. "Did you get shot as well?" Brian asked.

Chip had not even realized that his leg was bleeding. "No, I'm okay," Chip said. "I ripped my leg open on some barbed wire at the compound but the doctor stitched it up."

Michael grabbed a couple of tissues from a box on the end table and came over to give them to Chip. Chip quickly wiped the little bit of blood off of his leg. "You should be really proud of Eric," Michael said. "We'd probably all be dead if it wasn't for him and Maria." Michael turned toward Maria who was pacing back and forth just outside of the doors to the intensive care ward and waved her over to where they were sitting. "This is Maria," Michael said.

Brian tried to get up out of his chair to meet her, but it was only then that he realized how wobbly his legs were. Maria grabbed his hand and held him steady as she gave him a hug. "Pleased to meet you sir. I've heard so much about you."

Suddenly the door of the intensive care unit swung open. "He's awake now," the nurse said. "He'd like to see you." They all started toward the door. "Whoa, hold on," the nurse said. "One at a time and family only."

"You go first," Chip said to his father.

Brian slowly walked down the hallway toward Eric's bed with the nurse leading the way. "You can only stay for a few minutes," she said. "He's lost a lot of blood and we thought we were going to lose him there for a while, but he's a fighter."

Brian hated being in hospitals and the sight of tubes and blood always freaked him out so he steeled himself for what he was about to see. Despite that, he still wasn't prepared to see how frail and pale Eric looked. His skin almost had a blue tinge to it and it reminded him of when Eric was born. When he was born, Brian had thought there must have been something wrong because he was so blue, not the pink-skinned baby he was expecting.

"Hi Eric," Brian said as he touched his hand. He was shocked at how cold Eric's hand felt.

Eric slowly opened his eyes. "Hi Dad," Eric said. "I hope I don't look as bad as you do." Brian didn't realize that he looked almost as pale as Eric. "I guess I had you a bit worried, but don't be concerned, I'm going to be alright."

As Brian held his son's hand, you could almost see the colour come back into both of them at the same time. "Is everyone else okay?" Eric asked.

"Yeah, I think so," Brian replied. "Chip's got a gash on

his leg but it's been stitched up. He'll be coming in to see you in a few minutes. They said you're only allowed to have one visitor at a time."

"What about Maria?" Eric asked.

"I just met her out in the waiting room. She looked like she was okay. Everyone is worried about you."

"Was I the only one shot?"

"Yeah, and it turns out you were shot by a bloody U.S. marine who got a little trigger-happy."

"Jacob and Emily had always said their dad would be sending the marines to rescue us, "Eric said. "I guess they showed up a bit late but, I didn't know who they were when they came bursting out of the forest. They probably shot me because I had a gun. I had a feeling that gun was going to hurt me more than help me."

"It's not your fault son. I think the General knows that, because he's the one who flew me back to Rio on a military plane."

Eric tried to shift in his bed but the movement caused him to wince in pain. "I should go," Brian said. "Your brother wants to come in to see you." He gave his son a kiss on the forehead before he left.

"Is he okay?" Chip asked as Brian came through the doors back into the waiting room.

"Yeah, he's in a lot of pain but I think he's going to be alright," Brian said. "You can go see him now."

Chip headed through the doors into the intensive care ward. Brian could see Maria hovering in the background listening to everything he had said to Chip. "He asked if you were okay," Brian said to Maria.

"Oh, I'm fine," Maria said. "He's the one who got shot. I don't know why he'd be worried about me."

Brian smiled at her. Brian was starting to realize that Maria was more than just another hostage. It was only a few minutes later when Chip emerged from the intensive care unit. "He wants to see you," he said to Maria.

Maria started to head through the doors but was stopped by the nurse. "Sorry, but it's family members only," the nurse said. Maria immediately stopped in her tracks.

"She's part of the family," Chip said to the nurse. The nurse knew he was lying, but let Maria in anyway and led her to Eric's bed. As she followed behind, Maria suddenly felt very nervous. She never cried, but she had been crying a lot lately and she tried to wipe the tear stains from her face as she approached the bed. Eric had his eyes closed but opened them immediately when Maria touched his hand.

"You scared me," Maria said. "I thought I'd lost you."

"Not going to happen," Eric said, "although I might need someone to take care of me for a little while until I'm fully recovered. Do you know anyone who might want the job?"

"Possibly," Maria said as she pulled back the sheet to see the bandages that covered the hole just under his collar bone. "But that's a pretty nasty looking wound. You might need someone willing to stay with you around the clock and take care of your every need."

"I'm pretty sure that's exactly what I need," Eric said.

*** CHAPTER 32 ***

It was about a week later when Eric was deemed to be fit enough to leave the hospital and head back home to Canada. However, before they left the country, the Brazilian police wanted them to identify the suspected kidnappers they had rounded up since the incident. The other hostages had already been through the process, but there had been conflicting information given because the kidnappers had always wore masks or bandanas to cover their faces. The police were now bringing Eric, Chip, Michael and Maria in to see if they could identify the kidnappers. Brian accompanied them because he wasn't going to head home this time without taking his sons with him.

Michael was the first one led in to view the suspected kidnappers. "Remember, this is one way glass so they can't see you," the Brazilian police officer said to Michael. The door opened and ten suspects were led into the room on the other side of the glass. They were all dressed like the kidnappers had been dressed and had bandanas covering the lower parts of their faces. They all looked like kidnappers but Michael knew that some of them were policemen dressed up as kidnappers. Michael studied the eyes of each of the suspects.

"Please remove the bandanas," the police officer said into an intercom connected to the other room. As soon as Michael saw his face, he knew the man he had seen while looking underneath his hood as he lay in the back of the truck.

"Number three," Michael said. "He was the guard in the back of the truck as we were being driven out of the forest."

"Are you sure?" the police officer asked.

"Yes, absolutely sure. That's a face that I'll remember for the rest of my life."

"Are there any others?" the officer asked.

"I can't be sure about any of the others, but number three was definitely one of the kidnappers."

The procedure was repeated next with Chip, but he couldn't confirm the identity of any of the kidnappers. He thought one of the suspects looked like the doctor, but he wasn't sure. "They wore masks the entire time I saw them," Chip said, "so I can't be sure. I'm sorry."

Eric was the next one to view the suspects. He immediately focused in on one of the suspects as he was quite sure he was the doctor. But there was another man in the lineup that so closely resembled him that Eric was sure they were brothers. Eric didn't know what to do. "Number six and number eight both look a lot like the doctor, but I can't say for sure."

Maria was the next to be led in to see the suspects. She immediately recognized the doctor. She remembered his kind eyes from the way he had treated the injured hostages. She also remembered his face from when he saved her from being raped by the guards. "No, I don't recognize any of them," she said.

"Are you sure?" the police officer said. "You're the only one who saw the doctor without his mask on. The other hostages thought he might have been number six or number eight."

Maria focused in on number six again. She could still see kindness in his eyes. "No, the doctor isn't there. I'll remember his face for the rest of my life."

Maria was led back into the main meeting room where all of the others waited. They were going to do one last video conference with all of the police forces to give an update. This update would also be appearing on newscasts around the world. As they were waiting for the video conference to start, Chip pulled the gold medal from his pocket. "I believe this belongs to you," Chip said as he put it around Michael's neck. This time, Michael didn't hide it under his shirt.

As the TV screens lit up in the room, Brian recognized the FBI headquarters in Houston and could see Detective Mitchell and Detective Johnson on the screen. He also saw Elizabeth Noble and Kevin and Lisa Porter sitting in the background. The Porters were anxiously awaiting their son's return to the United States. Elizabeth Noble now knew that Brian had been responsible for paying the ransoms for the release of the last remaining hostages and she was pleased to see that both of Brian's kids were now safe.

"We'd like to give an update on the status of our investigation," the Brazilian police chief said. "We've charged six people with kidnapping including the tour guide and several suspected gunmen. We have had a hostage confirm the identity of one of gunmen and we have a strong case against the others based on other evidence. We are also pleased to report that Eric Baxter, the hostage that was shot during a rescue attempt has now been released from hospital and will be returning home to Canada later today." The camera panned to show Eric sitting with Brian, Chip, Michael and Maria.

Brian asked if he could say something and the Brazilian police chief slid the microphone over in front of him. "I'd like to thank Detective Mitchell for his work on this case and I'd especially like to thank Detective Johnson for the support he gave me during this difficult ordeal."

"We're just doing our job," Detective Mitchell said.

"Thank you," Detective Johnson said as he leaned into the microphone. "I'm so pleased to hear that your sons have been returned to you safely."

As soon as they heard his voice, Eric and Chip looked at each other in amazement. They both recognized his voice.

The Brazilian police chief wrapped up the video conference and the TV screens went black. "Chief," Eric said to the police chief. "We think we know another one of the people involved. The last detective who spoke was the one who was on the call with the kidnappers when we paid the additional six and a half million in ransom money. He was the one who gave us the account number to transfer the money to."

"Are you sure?" the police chief said.

Eric and Chip looked at each other. "Absolutely sure," they both said.

Brian felt utterly betrayed. "He was the one who encouraged me to pay the ransom when Detective Mitchell was advising against it," Brian said. "I was praising him for being so sympathetic about doing whatever was necessary to get my sons back. But now I realize he was just manipulating me to pay the ransom."

The Brazilian police chief immediately picked up the phone. "Get me Detective Mitchell at FBI headquarters in

Houston."

* * *

Brian, Eric and Chip sat in the waiting room at the Houston airport. They had completed the first leg of their journey home, flying from Rio to Houston, and were now waiting to board their flight back to Toronto. Brian was surprised to see Detective Mitchell walking toward them in the airport. "Detective Mitchell, I didn't expect to see you here," Brian said to him as he approached.

"I wanted to meet your two sons," Detective Mitchell said, "and give you a status update on our investigation." Brian introduced him to Eric and Chip. "I'd like you to know that we pressed charges against Detective Johnson about two hours ago. After our initial investigation, we confirmed that he was, in fact, the person you heard on the phone when talking with the kidnappers. We've also found out that he was the person who contacted the sports management company to get them to pay the ransom for Michael Porter."

"Why would he do that?" Brian asked.

"Money, of course," Detective Mitchell said. "As you know, he was secretly encouraging people to pay the ransoms for their family members. We found out he has been working with the kidnappers for quite some time, even before this latest incident. He was on the FBI team that was involved in the negotiations for the release of several oil and gas executives who have been kidnapped over the last few years. We've only now realized that he has been working with the kidnappers the whole time."

"Any chance our father will get back any of the ransom money he paid?" Eric asked the detective.

"Not any time soon, if ever," the detective said. "We've been trying to trace the money but most of it has already disappeared. We think the kidnappers have quite a network of corrupt bankers and lawyers who know how to launder the money. There may also be other police detectives involved. The Brazilian police chief said they already know there's a lot of corruption within their police force."

The detective thanked them for their assistance in the investigation and wished them well in their journey back to Canada.

"Sorry Dad," Eric said as they heard the boarding call for their flight.

"Sorry for what?" Brian asked.

"I guess we blew your entire legacy," Eric said.

Brian just smiled and gave both his sons a hug. "You've done nothing of the sort."

*** CHAPTER 33 ***

One month later...

Tom Beamish tried to hide how nervous he felt as he listened to his lawyer give his summary to the team of investigators who were reviewing his recent suspicious financial transactions, but the continual shifting in his chair and wringing of his hands was apparent to everyone in the room. At this stage, this was just an inquiry but Tom knew that he could be facing some hefty fines and possibly criminal charges as a result of their findings. He had asked John Bancroft, a highly respected lawyer and a personal friend, to help him through this ordeal.

"As you are aware," Mr. Bancroft said, "the guidelines identify several different categories of deceptive activities that could lead to sanctions against my client. Clearly there is no criminal element of fraud, forgery or theft as my client did not use the funds for personal use and exploitation. Mr. Baxter has provided you with his statement that he instructed my client to cash out his holdings to pay the ransom for the safe release of his two sons and several other people." Mr. Bancroft showed a picture of all of the people that had been rescued. "All of these people are alive today due to the actions of my client." He paused to make sure the panel members could see the faces of the people rescued.

Next, Mr. Bancroft held up two statements that he had obtained from Mr. McKenzie and Mr. Ronson. It was their money that had been sitting in the trust account that Tom had used as part of the funds to pay the ransom. "Both Mr. Johnson and Mr. Ronson have indicated they suffered no financial loss due to my client's actions. Both have been fully compensated for any interest lost while their funds were used to pay the ransom before their money was replaced when the markets opened the next morning. Furthermore, both have agreed that the circumstances justified the activities of my client."

"Yes, but your client did not obtain their permission to perform those activities ahead of time," one of the panel members interrupted, "only after the fact."

"Agreed," Mr. Bancroft said, "but I would argue that a defence of necessity should be applied in this situation."

"Defence of necessity?" the panel member asked.

"Yes, that's where an act that would normally be considered a criminal activity is justified based on a life or lives being in imminent peril. For example, if I broke into a hardware store to get a ladder to rescue someone on the second floor of a burning building, that would be considered a defence of necessity. I would argue that my client meets the criteria for that defence. The lives of the hostages were clearly in danger and my client could not wait to obtain the necessary permissions to use those funds, or else the lives of the hostages would have been lost." Mr. Bancroft could tell from the expressions on the faces of those on the panel that they agreed that the ends justified the means in this situation.

"In addition to this," continued Mr. Bancroft, "there is clearly no misappropriation of funds because there was no benefit to my client whatsoever."

"Yes, but what about the misapplication of funds?" the same panel member interrupted again. It was clear he was the panel member that they were going to have the hardest time convincing. "That's where funds were improperly used for the benefit of a third party. I believe that element applies in this situation."

"Agreed," Mr. Bancroft said, "but your own guidelines identify six specific factors that must be considered. We've already satisfied the first four factors. There was no financial benefit to my client by these actions, so that satisfies the fifth element. And lastly, my client did not attempt to conceal his activities from the authorities."

"Not completely," the panel member said. "We've never received a full explanation as to where the other three and a half million dollars was obtained."

Mr. Bancroft had hoped that the investigative panel would have missed the one element in their defence where they were most vulnerable. Tom had never revealed where he had obtained the last three and half million dollars required to pay the ransom, not even to his lawyer. He was not going to reveal that Randy, the person who had helped him start his career as a financial planner, was the person he had called in his time of need. There was no point taking Randy down with him at this point.

"All I can say to that," Mr. Bancroft said, "is that my client promised not to reveal who provided him those funds and he is standing by that promise. I believe my client's actions has saved multiple lives, he has not gained any personal benefit from these actions and no one has been harmed by these actions. My client has had a long and distinguished career in the financial services industry and I believe he should be viewed as a hero in this situation. We believe your decision in this matter should reflect that."

The investigative panel looked at each other to see if they had any other questions. "Thank you for your attendance today," the lead panelist said. "We will be issuing the results of our review within the next ten days."

* * *

Chip opened his mailbox at Ohio State University and saw the envelope that identified that it was from the Awards and Scholarships department. He had a feeling that he would be receiving this letter and he wasn't looking forward to it. He stuffed the letter into his backpack and headed off to his dorm room. When he got there, he stared at the letter for several minutes before he opened it. He took a big breath as he quickly skipped over the preamble and jumped down to the important parts.

"As a result of your recently discovered medical condition and the medications required to treat this condition, it has been determined that you will not be permitted to compete in Big Ten Conference athletic events while undergoing treatment."

Chip knew this was coming because the medications used to treat his Crohn's disease involved the use of steroids. However, the next sentence almost knocked the wind out of him.

"Since the ability to compete in athletic events is a condition of the scholarship award, we regret to inform you that we can no longer offer you a full scholarship at Ohio State."

Chip had no idea how he was going to be able to afford to complete his last year at Ohio State. He knew his father had used all of his money to pay the ransoms, so there was no money left in the "Bank of Dad". Chip threw himself back on his bed and stared at the ceiling. He thought about approaching his brother to see if he could help, but decided against it because he knew Eric had just started his new job and wouldn't have any extra money sitting around.

Chip sat up and turned to the next page of the letter. It showed the tuition fees for the coming year would be about $25,000. In addition, there was another $10,000 for room and board, plus money for books, living expenses and health insurance. In total, the estimated costs were about $44,000.

Chip flipped forward a few pages to try to see when they would require their first payment. As he did so, a brochure fell from the package and landed on the floor. Chip noticed that it had a hand-written note from his coach attached to it.

"We'd all really like you to complete your last year here at Ohio State. This brochure contains information about a new scholarship that has just been announced to be given to those athletes who sacrifice their own personal goals for the benefit of their teammates. I think you have a very good chance of winning!!!"

Chip looked at the brochure and could see the familiar logo of a major sports company. The brochure indicated it was an annual award of $25,000. It wouldn't cover everything, but it would certainly help.

When he turned to the last page of the brochure, it became apparent why his coach thought Chip had a good chance of winning. On it was a picture of Chip and Michael Porter as they walked off the track arm in arm at the Olympics.

*** CHAPTER 34 ***

Brian was in his kitchen cleaning up after lunch when he heard a knock on his front door. "Coming," he shouted as he wiped his hands on one of the dish towels. "Elizabeth, this is a surprise," he said when he saw Elizabeth Noble standing there when he opened the door.

"I don't mean to intrude," Elizabeth said, "but I wanted to deliver this to you in person."

"Come in, come in, you're not intruding," Brian said as he led her into his living room. "What exactly are you delivering?"

Elizabeth sat on the edge of the couch. "This," she said handing Brian an envelope. Brian opened the envelope to see a cheque made out to him for a million dollars. "I wanted to pay you back for the ransom you paid to have my Sylvia released by the kidnappers. We should have paid it ourselves."

Brian stared at the cheque not knowing what to say.

"Peter and I are getting a divorce," Elizabeth confessed. "I just couldn't stay with a man who wouldn't pay the ransom to have his own daughter released. There are things more important than money. I'm not sure she'll ever forgive me, but I'm trying to reconnect with my daughter. Next week, she's agreed to let me meet my grandchildren." Elizabeth pulled a tissue out of her purse to wipe away a tear that was trickling down her cheek.

"I'm sure she'll forgive you," Brian said. "Just give her some time."

"Well, I've taken up enough of your time," Elizabeth said as she rose from the couch. "I'm so glad to hear that both of your sons are okay."

"Would you like to meet them?" Brian asked. "We're getting together for dinner tonight."

"No, I wouldn't want to impose," Elizabeth said. She gave Brian a hug. "You're so lucky to have your family."

Brian watched her as she headed back to the taxi she had waiting for her. He wondered if there was anything else he could have said to convince her to join them all at their dinner that evening.

* * *

Eric was sitting at his desk going through the mountain of emails that were sitting in his inbox. There were a lot of emails from friends saying how happy they were to hear that he and Chip had been saved from the kidnappers. Many of the emails had questions asking what it was like to be kidnapped and Eric felt obligated to respond to them all. He had already been working on responding to the emails for a couple of weeks.

When he opened the next email, he realized it had been sent before the whole kidnapping ordeal had started. The email was from one of the *Banff Babes*, the friends of his mother. She had responded to Eric's request for information as to what his parents' legacy could be.

"I know exactly what your parents' legacy is," the email

said. "Please call me when you get this email and I'll explain it to you," the email continued and it gave the telephone number to call.

"Eureka!" Eric said as he pulled out his cell phone to call. Unfortunately, the call went to voice-mail. Eric looked at his watch and realized he had run out of time. His mother's birthday supper would be starting shortly and he knew he couldn't be late.

* * *

"Thanks for coming," Brian said to Tom Beamish as he came walking through the door of the restaurant.

"I wouldn't miss one of Jean's birthday suppers for the world," Tom said. He recalled the many happy times they had had over the years. Jean's birthday suppers used to be known as quite the parties with lots of people attending. Tom wondered why Brian continued to have them after Jean passed away but he felt honoured to be invited every year. It was his way to stay connected with Eric and Chip.

As they stood there waiting for the others to arrive, Brian couldn't help wondering whether Tom had heard the results of the investigation yet. "So, any word yet?" Brian asked.

Tom knew exactly what he was talking about. "Yeah, my lawyer and I just met with them today. They said they wouldn't be pursuing any criminal charges or imposing any fines."

"That's great!" Brian said.

"Yeah, but it wasn't all good news. They wanted to suspend me for a year for misapplication of funds. They said if I agreed to just retire from the business, they'd drop the matter."

"Are you going to fight it?" Brian asked.

"No, it's about time I retired and passed the business on

197

to my partners. It's something I've been thinking of doing for a while anyway."

"I don't understand why they'd want to suspend you," Brian said. "You didn't gain anything from this."

"Financially, no," Tom said. "But I actually gained quite a bit from it – I got your two boys back safe and sound."

They both looked at each other knowing it was all worth it and they'd do it all again. They turned as they saw Eric coming through the door.

"Hi Dad," Eric said. "I hope you don't mind but I brought Maria along with me."

"Maria," Brian said giving her a hug. "It's so good to see you again. What brings you up to Canada?"

"Maria's been accepted into the nursing program at George Brown College," Eric said. "I figured that since she did such a good job taking care of us at the compound, I'd encourage her to apply to pursue it as her career."

"Are you sure you didn't have any ulterior motives?" Brian asked.

"Well, I suppose there might be a bit of an upside for me as well," Eric confessed.

"You better watch out for him," Brian whispered to Maria. "He might be trying to lead you astray."

"Yeah, I thought of that," Maria said, "but I'm keeping my eye on him."

"Okay, everyone's here except Chip," Brian said. "That son of mine is late for everything. If he's not here in five minutes, we'll start without him." Brian took another look at his watch. "We've got a private room reserved for our supper tonight," Brian said, pointing to a private little room that had stained glass doors separating it from the main part of the restaurant.

"Excuse me sir," the hostess said when she overheard Brian, "but I believe your other son has been here for quite some time." The hostess led the way to the private room and opened the glass doors to reveal Chip and a young woman sitting at the table. Brian didn't recognize the woman.

"Hi Dad, this is Robin," Chip said as they both rose from their seats. "I met Robin at the Olympics, as she was on the Canadian team. I knew we shouldn't have gotten here early, but Robin's a stickler about being on time."

"Nice to meet you," Brian said as he shook her hand. "I've been trying to get Chip to be punctual for years, without any success. What's your secret?"

"She just leaves without me if I'm late," Chip interjected.

"If you snooze, you lose," Robin teased. Brian instantly like her.

They spent over two hours enjoying Jean's birthday celebration supper. Brian told stories about the good times they'd had over the years, including a few embarrassing stories about Eric and Chip when they were kids. Eric and Chip had heard many of these stories before but it still felt good to recall them. But every year, their father seemed to come up with at least one new one that they'd never heard before. Robin found a few more things to tease Chip about and Maria loved the feeling of being part of such a family.

"Well, I guess we've come to the part of the evening where I reveal the details of my legacy," Brian said, "unless you've already figured it out," he continued, looking at Eric.

"It's sort of a moot point, isn't it Dad?" Eric said. "I believe the kidnappers made off with your legacy."

"You still don't get it," Brian said. "But it's not a moot point at all," he said pulling out the cheque he had received earlier that day. "Elizabeth Noble gave me a cheque today for a million dollars to reimburse me for the ransom I paid for her daughter's release. But a legacy is not about the money. Leaving a legacy is about leaving things better than they were before and I believe your mother and I have built a huge legacy."

"I don't understand," Eric said.

"Estúpido," Maria said under her breath.

"I don't speak Portuguese, but even I know what estúpido means," Eric said turning toward her.

Maria blushed with embarrassment. "Sorry, I didn't mean to say that out loud, but surely you must know what your father's legacy is."

Eric and Chip looked at each other confused.

"You are," she said to them. "He's leaving his two sons behind as his legacy."

"You better hang on to her son," Brian said. "She's a keeper."

* * *

Later that night Brian looked through some old family albums as he lay in bed, recalling some of the past birthday celebrations that he'd had with Jean. Slowly he drifted off to sleep.

"Thanks for the birthday party," Jean said to him in his dream.

"You're welcome," Brian said.

"But you should probably stop having them. I've been dead for six years now. It's time to move on."

"What's it to you? Don't you like birthday parties where you don't actually get any older?"

"You have a point, but it's still time to move on. Elizabeth Noble seems nice. She's pretty and now that she's getting a divorce, I thought you might want to pursue her."

"Why would I want to do that?" Brian said. "I've already had the love of my life. No one can replace you."

"That's sweet of you to say, but I don't want you to be

alone. Besides, I think she's going to be pretty rich after her divorce."

"It's only money," Brian said.

"Yeah, but you don't have any," Jean said. "You're going to give away most of that million dollar cheque, aren't you? What are you going to live on?"

"Well, Eric put some money in some mutual funds for me and I plan to use some of the money I got from Elizabeth Noble to top it up. It's not much, but it's enough to meet my needs. And I've already got all of my wants."

"I think you underestimate how much money you'll need to retire," Jean said.

"Maybe," Brian said, "but I wanted to pay for Tom's legal fees because he put himself out on a limb to get the money to rescue the boys. I also wanted to give some money to Chip so he could finish off his last year at Ohio State. Even with the scholarship, he's going to need more money to finish off his degree and he's talking about getting his MBA someday. I know how much you wanted the boys to get a good education. And Maria's practically family now so I thought I should help pay for her to get her nursing degree because she doesn't have any money and doesn't qualify for any student loans."

"Leaving a legacy really is your most important objective," Jean said.

Brian rolled over in the bed so he could look into Jean's eyes. "Absolutely. Have I told you lately that I love you?"

"Not for the longest time," Jean said.

"Well, I do," Brian said. "I love you passionately."

"I love you passionately too," Jean said.

As he slept, a small smile appeared on Brian's face. "So exactly how rich did you say Elizabeth Noble is?"

"I didn't," Jean said. "Just go to sleep dear."

Other Books By

E.A. Briginshaw

Goliath

Henry Shaw leads a relatively quiet life trying to balance his work at a growing law firm with his family life, including supporting his teenage son who has a promising soccer career ahead of him. But all of that changes when Henry's bipolar brother, in one of his manic states, tells him that Goliath didn't really die as told in the biblical story – and that he is Goliath.

When his brother disappears along with a media magnate, the FBI and the local police believe they may have been part of a secret international network and that Goliath was his brother's code name. The solution to this puzzle may reside in his brother's laptop computer, which mysteriously disappears during a break-in at his house.

Is his brother dead or just hiding from forces trying to destroy the network? Henry tries to solve the puzzle along with an intriguing woman he encounters at an airport bar.

Goliath is available for purchase on the Amazon.com website.
Book   (ISBN 978-0-9921390-0-1)
eBook (ISBN 978-0-9921390-1-8)

34469006R00126

Made in the USA
Charleston, SC
10 October 2014